Two Birds With
One Scone

Katy Lee

Annie's®
AnniesFiction.com

Books in the Chocolate Shoppe Mysteries series

Library of Congress-in-Publication Data
Two Birds With One Scone / by Katy Lee
p. cm.
ISBN: 979-8-89253-017-0
I. Title
                2018930159

AnniesFiction.com
(800) 282-6643
Chocolate Shoppe Mysteries™
Series Creator: Shari Lohner
Series Editor: Elizabeth Morrissey
Cover Illustrator: Bonnie Leick

10 11 12 13 14 | Printed in China | 9 8 7 6 5

1

Jillian Green took a deep breath and slowly released the white sugar flower she'd molded to mimic the magnolia blossoms bursting forth throughout Moss Hollow, Georgia.

She was going to call these gum-paste decorations "sugared magnolias," inspired by the ornamental branches gracefully adorning the sidewalk outside The Chocolate Shoppe Bakery. She hoped that the tiny, sweet reproductions would become a local favorite for wedding, baby shower, and birthday cakes. Maybe they would even be a tourist draw when they topped cupcakes in the display case.

Jillian had worked hard for the last few years proving to her grandmother, Bertie Harper, that she was up to the challenge of someday running the business. With lots of practice—and plenty of instruction from Bertie and The Chocolate Shoppe's veteran master baker, Lenora Ryan—Jillian had become quite competent at most pastries, pies, cookies, breads, and other goodies, but she was beginning to think that her true gift was for cake decorating.

That is, she was beginning to think so until she realized she couldn't keep her sugared magnolias from drooping in the June heat.

The back door slammed.

The petals sagged.

Jillian sighed in defeat. She'd been practicing for days and still couldn't convince them to maintain their shape. She glanced up over her wilted creation and forced a smile at her grandmother, who stood in the doorway.

"That flower looks better than the ones you made yesterday,"

Bertie said in her Southern drawl. She squinted and cocked her head. "I think it does, anyway. What is this, your third try?"

Jillian grimaced. "Sixth. But thanks for not counting, Bertie."

"Why the long face?" the eightysomething blonde beauty asked. "I once read that Einstein supposedly said that anyone who has never made a mistake never tried anything new."

Jillian pulled plastic gloves off her hands and tossed them into the trash. "Interesting, because, apparently, he also said the definition of insanity is doing the same thing over and over again and expecting different results. At least that's what I've read and seen plastered all over pictures on social media. And I might have even seen it on a poster in a shop at the mall once. But can you really trust anything you find on the Internet? I mean—"

"Hush, child. How's a person to get a word in edgewise with you chattering on like that?"

Jillian knew she was chattering, but Bertie was wearing her "I'm about to set you straight" face. Jillian remembered seeing the same look more than a few other times in the past. The first time had been when she'd taken Jillian in after her final year of high school—but then it had been aimed at Jillian's free-spirited parents, who had sold their tiny bungalow on the outskirts of Moss Hollow and then bought a travel trailer, departing for roads less traveled and leaving Jillian behind in the process.

A life of no destination hadn't been what Jillian wanted. A life without her grandmother wasn't either, but college had beckoned. Bertie had graciously sent her off to California, where Jillian had spent twenty years, enjoying a successful career in advertising after graduating from college. But then a personal crisis involving an embezzling fiancé had shown Jillian the truth: Moss Hollow would always be her home.

Now, Bertie peered at the failed flowers, her piercing blue eyes missing nothing.

"Aunt Cornelia has some idea that I am somehow 'blocking the flow of my art,' whatever that means," Jillian said. "I don't know what I'm doing wrong, Bertie, but I'm frustrated enough that I'm starting to consider her fanciful theory."

"Did someone say fanciful?" The swinging door that led to the front of the bakery opened wide. "You must have been talking about me." Cornelia Montgomery, Bertie's twin sister, breezed into the kitchen, carrying the scent of peach blossoms with her. "Fanciful is just one of the many words to describe me."

Bertie snorted. "I can think of a few others." She lifted her chin with a quick sniff. "Perfect timing, however. Jillian was just showing off her latest creation."

Cornelia's nose wrinkled at the sight of the lump of sugar. "Is that supposed to be eaten, dear?"

Jillian scooped up the limp flower and tossed it into the trash. "Technically, yes. But I wouldn't feed this to Possum." *That cat is addicted to bacon anyway.*

Cornelia waved her hand dramatically in front of her face. "I'm sure Raymond thanks you. No offense, of course." Cornelia insisted that her late husband, Raymond, lived on through her sister's cat, Possum.

"No offense taken. Now, what brings you ladies here after hours?" Jillian busied herself cleaning up her mess as the twin sisters pulled up a couple chairs. *Are they planning to stay awhile?* "And can it wait until I get home? I'd like to clean up, lock up, and forget about this afternoon." Jillian's bedroom at Belle Haven, the quintessential Southern mansion she shared with Bertie and Cornelia, was calling to her. It was a bit too warm for a fire in the fireplace, but a glass of sweet tea and a good book from the library sounded like just what the doctor ordered.

"This can't wait, my dear," Jillian's grandmother said solemnly. Even Cornelia's typical exuberance faded, and Jillian's heart pounded with anxiety. *This must be serious.* Jillian eyed them both. "Should I expect my walking papers?"

"Don't even joke like that." Bertie wagged her finger. "You know that would never happen."

"So why the serious faces? Did someone die?" The idea caught Jillian's breath in her chest. "Oh, no, that's it, isn't it? Someone died. Who?"

"No one died," Bertie said, leaning back in her chair.

"Not yet, anyway." Cornelia cackled gleefully, her trademark mirth returning. "But when you find out what we've signed you up for, your handsome beau might be handling a twin burial at his funeral home."

Jillian felt her cheeks turn pink. Hearing Hunter Greyson called her beau still brought a smile to her face—and threatened to make her lose her focus on the matter at hand. She shook her head. "Don't beat around the bush, you two. What exactly have you gotten me into?" A heavy feeling of dread weighed down on her.

"Do you want to sit?" Cornelia asked.

"Just spill it, please." Remaining standing, Jillian crossed her arms impatiently.

Bertie cleared her throat. "There's no easy way to say this, so I'll just come right out with it. We signed up the bakery to cater the Moss Hollow Arts Commission's Sweet Sounds fund-raiser. On Saturday."

"Today is Thursday," Jillian said. A little more prep time would have been nice, but she knew they could fit in the extra work. The real challenge would be making sure everything went off without a hitch at the event, but she and Bertie had catered enough events together that they had their rhythm down. "Why the late notice?"

"The commission's previous caterer came down with some type of illness—it sounded quite nasty, according to my friend in the garden club—and I answered the call for help," Cornelia said.

"I mean, really, you don't turn down an opportunity to help out the richest woman in Nathan County."

Bertie snorted. "My sister may not own this bakery, but she certainly has no problem volunteering its services."

"You said you thought it was a good idea, Bertie. Don't go making this my fault." Cornelia turned pleading eyes to Jillian. "You wouldn't want some caterer from Atlanta sneezing and coughing all over those rich folks' fancy desserts, now would you?"

"Of course not," Jillian said, "but why would I find catering a fund-raiser unsettling enough to warrant a call to the coroner for you two? We've done desserts at plenty of—wait . . ." Jillian's stomach took a nosedive and her knees went weak. "Aren't you two attending the church retreat Saturday with Lenora? How will you be in two places at once?"

Forced twin smiles beamed her way. The picture became clear.

Jillian glared first at her great-aunt, then her grandmother. "You won't be at the fund-raiser, which means you're sending me on a solo flight. Am I right?"

"Buck up, Jillian." Bertie clapped her hands together. "It's only dessert for 200 people. I believe in you."

Jillian swallowed hard. "Two . . . hundred?"

Bertie waved her hand dismissively and continued with her pep talk. "You have a tough streak in you. You may get knocked down, but you don't stay down. You get back up on your feet and do what it takes to come out on top."

"Did you memorize a book of affirmations on the way here?" Jillian asked.

"No need to get fresh when I'm being supportive, young lady," Bertie said. "Take these little sugar flowers, for example. Would you have ever thought in your swanky advertising agency out in California that you'd be staying well past store hours trying to perfect a wedding cake decoration? Or that it would be vastly more fulfilling than making commercials for dish soap?"

Jillian sighed. "No, I don't suppose I would have thought that. I also never thought my fiancé would turn out to be a criminal and ruin my career by association."

"You can't blame yourself for that, dear," Cornelia said. "David Drake was distractingly handsome for a scoundrel."

Bertie rose from her chair and came beside Jillian. "All that's in the past, Jillian. Everybody makes mistakes or errors in judgment. It's about whether you learn and grow from them or let them drag you down. And you are a trooper. Always have been. Don't ever doubt your ability to handle anything—including a ritzy catered affair."

Jillian groaned in frustration. "I can't even get these darn flowers to hold and you want me to take on serving 200 people alone?"

"This will be an opportunity to shine. Besides, you're not alone right now. You're going to put on a spread to die for, and we're going to help."

"Until the bus leaves Moss Hollow Community Church in thirty-six hours anyway," Cornelia chimed in.

"Not helpful, Sister," Bertie scolded, then turned back to Jillian. "The highfalutin members of the arts commission will never again order desserts from anyone else for their ritzy events, mark my words."

"But if we're shifting gears to highfalutin desserts, what about the cake flowers?" Jillian asked.

Bertie put a finger to her chin in thought. "I've got a hunch you're not letting your gum paste mature long enough. Are your petals extra fragile and not holding up?"

Jillian huffed. "You could say that."

"You need a good twenty-four hours before the paste is ready to be manipulated. It needs time to cure. Remember, good things come to those who wait. I've also got a hunch that this fund-raiser will bring many good things your way."

Jillian's shoulders relaxed a little. Bertie had always been her champion, even if she had to knock some sense into Jillian in the process. At any age, whether at seventeen or forty, Jillian knew this woman would always come to her aid.

Except for this Saturday. Jillian's shoulders tensed right back up. If any problems arose at the event, she would be on her own. But not tonight. "What's on the menu first?"

"Scones. Raspberry almond, to be exact," Cornelia said. "It's a special request from Lucinda Atwood. She's the commission chairwoman, and she's hosting the fund-raiser at Jardin d'Amandes."

"Garden of almonds?" Jillian screwed up her face at the somewhat odd estate name. "I thought almonds don't grow in Georgia."

"They don't, dear," Cornelia said, "but the man who named it didn't know that. Glendon Powell was a poor Yankee boy who struck it rich in the California gold rush. Had enough money to burn a wet mule. He was visiting Atlanta after that, and he fell in love with a local girl. They lived in California for a while, but the girl missed home something fierce, so he bought her the biggest house in the county. Named it Jardin d'Amandes and even had a big old marble obelisk put up out front with the name carved right in it."

"Sounds like true love to me," Jillian said.

Cornelia nodded, clearly relishing her storytelling. "Apparently when they lived out West, the wife had developed quite an affection for almonds—ate them on darn near everything—so that fool man promised her they'd have the biggest almond orchard in Georgia."

"Seems to me he was the biggest nut in Georgia," Bertie muttered.

Cornelia ignored her and continued. "Well, turns out Glendon knew absolutely nothing about growing almond trees, or farming in general for that matter. He tried for ten years, but he couldn't grow a single tree, let alone an orchard. Ruined the land in the process too. And he ended up empty-handed in more ways than one—his sweet wife skipped town with his fortune, and poor Glendon lost the house and was left with not one almond to his name."

"That's a terrible story," Jillian said. "I'm surprised none of the subsequent owners changed the name of the estate."

"Perhaps they all thought it wise to remember the folly of previous generations," Bertie said sagely.

"Or they just didn't want to remove that twenty-ton obelisk," Cornelia said. "The entire orchard was sold off bit by bit to accommodate new houses, but none of them is as breathtaking as the mansion at Jardin d'Amandes." She pronounced the name with an especially dramatic French accent and fluttered an imaginary fan in front of her face. "Anyway, I know for a fact that Lucinda Atwood loves her almonds, which is probably why she never changed the name either. And that's why she requested these raspberry almond scones for the fund-raiser."

"Speaking of which, let's get back to the work at hand, shall we?" Bertie donned an apron. "We can make the scone dough today and bake them on Saturday before the fund-raiser."

"You mean *I* can bake them on Saturday," Jillian muttered. After a breath, she resolved to be more positive. "Remember when my scones used to be rock hard? They could only use them in batting practice down at the Little League field."

"Or skipping them across the creek at that house Hunter's fixing up." Bertie pinned up her blonde hair in a hairnet and passed one over to Cornelia to do the same.

"We tried that once," Jillian joked. They hadn't, not with a scone anyway, but they had had plenty of picnics on the property Hunter worked on in his spare time. She was looking forward to more of those picnics in the thick grass this summer, listening to the running water nearby.

A knock came at the bakery's front door, which had been locked since closing time a few hours prior. Before Jillian could wonder aloud who it might be, Cornelia said, "That'll be the Sweetie Pies. I'll let them in."

Cornelia disappeared through the kitchen door, then reappeared with every other member of the Southern Sweetie Pies baking club, who bustled in with boisterous voices and warm smiles.

"You all came out tonight to help me prep for this fund-raiser?" Jillian asked the swarming women. Her heart swelled at the sight of them.

"Of course," Savannah Cantrell replied on her way to place a hairnet over her dark shoulder-length hair. The town's favorite accountant, Jillian's best friend was a smart cookie—and had a gift for baking them as well. "As Sweetie Pies, it's our duty."

"And our pleasure," Laura Lee Zane added as she grabbed an apron from the rack on the wall. Although Laura Lee was no-nonsense when she was on the job as a sheriff's deputy, her friendly smile could also light up an entire room in an instant.

Her heart full of faith that the daunting task ahead of her was manageable, Jillian soldiered on as the Southern Sweetie Pies chatted and joked while they whipped up baked goods from scratch. Flour puffed through the air in a cloud and settled on the shoulders and noses of the members—Bertie, Cornelia, Savannah, Laura Lee, Annalise Reed, Lenora Ryan, Josi Rosenschein, Maudie Honeycutt, and Wanda Jean Maplewood. The help and time these women offered Jillian, asking nothing in return, filled her heart with gratitude.

Lenora, The Chocolate Shoppe's master baker who lived in an apartment above the shop, spoke up in her sassy tone. "The way y'all are throwing that flour about, I'll be surprised if we make half a batch." She laughed. "I'll be sweeping for days, but it's a small price to pay for Jillian saving our behinds."

A dimpled smiled bridged Annalise's chubby cheeks. "No one leaves here until the place is spotless. Not to worry, Lenora. We got you covered."

Everyone else agreed.

Jillian sent up a prayer of thanksgiving for such loving and considerate people in her life. Since welcoming her into the baking club when she returned to town, this group of lively women had shown Jillian time and time again that they considered her family. They made her feel at home.

Home sweet home.

"That scone dough looks perfect," Bertie said, inspecting the contents of Jillian's bowl. "Your days of hockey pucks are over."

A s Jillian restocked croissants in the display case Friday morning, a colorful poster taped to the bakery window caught her eye. The flyer had been there for weeks, she realized, but she hadn't paid it much attention until The Chocolate Shoppe had agreed to cater dessert for the event it advertised.

She walked across the bakery to give the poster a closer look. Half the page displayed a set of curving piano keys while the other half was filled with text so small she'd need a magnifying glass to read it.

"It's nice of Lucinda Atwood to open her home for this event, but with type so small, how will anyone know where it is?" she asked no one in particular. There were plenty of customers around, but they were all deep in their conversations and no one heard her rhetorical question. Except one rather special customer.

"Sounds like they should have consulted an advertising expert," Hunter Greyson responded as he stepped up behind Jillian, closing the newspaper he'd been reading as he studied the poster. "I know someone I could recommend. She's smart as a whip."

Jillian smiled at the compliment, then gestured to the poster. "I like how the curved piano keys indicate the flow of music, and the colors are nice. But that font is too fancy and it needs to be a few points bigger. I can't read it."

"It says the tickets are ridiculously expensive. I'll still be there, though."

"You will?"

"Of course. It's for a good cause. And Greyson & Sons is a longtime sponsor of the arts commission. We have a fund specifically for charitable donations."

"I didn't realize that. You're a man of hidden depths." Out of the corner of her eye, she beamed proudly at this handsome and considerate man. As he read the poster intently, he ran a hand through his thick dark hair, which was touched with hints of gray that gave him a distinguished air. The locks fell right back into perfect waves after he moved his hand away. Hunter was well-respected in Moss Hollow and could be called away at a moment's notice to his duties as the director of the Greyson & Sons Funeral Home, the family-owned business. He gave much to this town, whether with his time or his money.

He leaned closer to Jillian. "Word is that there will be a fantastic piano player there. The commission hired him to play with the school's jazz band. Should be a lively night."

"The arts commission isn't really known for its liveliness. How exciting could it be?"

He flashed her a grin, his bright blues capturing her. Hunter's eyes still gave her butterflies, but she was getting used to that by now.

She waited for his answer as if it would solve all the problems in the world. His easygoing manner and rugged good looks could encourage heads of state to sit down and listen to weather patterns with apt interest.

"So lively that there will be dancing." He wiggled his dark eyebrows.

"Dancing?" Her voice rose.

He nodded once. "Can I hope to have a spin around the floor with you?"

An image of being held in Hunter's arms as he glided her across marble tiles flashed in her mind. She agreed with a smile. Then she envisioned the other dancers clad in designer evening gowns, and the thought of her own baker's uniform, hairnet and all, brought the music in her daydream to a screeching halt.

Disappointed, Jillian shuffled back to the display case and swiped a rag across it as though Maggie, the bakery's countergirl, hadn't done it in weeks, when in actuality she'd cleaned it twice already that morning.

"Did I say something wrong?" Hunter approached the counter, a shadow of doubt flashed across his face. "We've danced before."

"I know. It's just that this time I'll be working, with a hairnet to boot. I won't be there to socialize. I'm not sure Lucinda Atwood would take kindly to the help dancing with her guests."

"I don't think I would have noticed the hairnet," Hunter protested, but she could tell he was trying not to grin.

"Liar, liar, tuxedo on fire," Jillian said with a laugh. "I think you would have noticed, but you would be too kind to comment on it."

"Guilty as charged." Hunter held up his hands in a gesture of admittance. "Anyway, what do you say?"

"About what?"

"About a dance. Remember, I was asking you to save me a dance, or two, or three."

Jillian snapped to attention. "Oh, right—a dance. I'm not sure."

"No one would mind. Trust me."

"I'm just worried about handling everything myself tomorrow night. Bertie and Cornelia are going to the church retreat, and they're taking every other Sweetie Pie over fifty with them. Savannah has plans and Laura Lee is working, so I'm on my own. No time for dancing." Jillian sighed as the front door jingled to announce the arrival of a new customer.

"We'll see about that," Hunter said, eyes twinkling. "Besides, you're forgetting that I'll be there. I can plate petits fours with the best of them. You can count on me to save the day."

"Fat chance of that!" A man's angry voice broke the connection between Jillian and Hunter in an abrupt second. "There won't be anyone to help you after I call my lawyer, lady. You are going to pay."

Hunter instantly put up a hand to keep the irate man from leaning any closer over the glass counter. Jillian hadn't even seen him approach.

A strong, fast flick of the man's wrist pushed Hunter's hand back at him. *Not a good move if Hunter's bright-blue eyes changing to storm clouds means anything.* Jillian quickly stepped around to the front of the display case and placed herself between the two men.

"What is this about?" she asked. "There must be a misunderstanding. I don't believe we've met."

The man appeared to be in his late twenties, but a small scar beneath his left eye indicated life hadn't been easy, despite the affluent air given off by his crisp polo shirt and Top-Sider shoes. "I was in here last week. Maybe you don't remember because I had my hair down." He twisted his head to one side to reveal a small blond ponytail at the nape of his neck.

Still, Jillian thought she would have remembered his face, especially with that scar. She shook her head. "We're a small town. We notice when someone is new."

"Doesn't matter. You'll be hearing from my attorney. You nearly killed me."

"What are you talking about?" Jillian was completely confounded.

"You sold me a cookie that had nuts in it. I specifically said I was allergic. I've been in the hospital for days."

Mixed emotions flooded her. On one hand, the man had a right to be angry for nearly dying from someone's negligence. But on the other, she knew that that someone was not her.

Was it Maggie? A deep sadness overtook Jillian at the thought of it being her trusted employee. "Are you sure it was me who sold the cookie to you?"

"Are you the owner?"

Now concern for Bertie stepped into Jillian's mind, putting her on the defensive. "Why does it matter who the owner is?" she asked, attempting to slow the conversation until she could get a read on his motive. She had to protect Bertie at all costs.

"Because the owner has the most to lose. I don't just want some employee getting fired and everything getting swept under the rug. I want heads to roll."

"Meaning he's looking to shut you down." Hunter turned to the man. "Let your attorney call. He can talk to ours." With that, Hunter herded the stranger toward the door. In one swoop, Hunter had the door open wide and the man over the threshold before the bell finished jingling. "Don't come around here again."

Grateful for his intervention, Jillian stepped up to the glass window overlooking Main Street. Friends and neighbors talking and laughing under the colorful striped awnings above the quaint storefronts didn't match the ire of the young man glaring back at her.

"Are you sure you never saw him before?" Hunter asked.

Jillian's throat was parched, so she gave a short nod. The man still stared at her, but his hand reached into his pocket and removed a cell phone. Before she could react, he lifted it and snapped a picture of her.

She leaped back in shock. *Why does he need my photo?* Did he need it so his attorney would know who to go after?

Jillian couldn't let her grandmother lose her livelihood. The Chocolate Shoppe Bakery was everything to Bertie.

"If I did sell him a cookie with nuts, I don't remember it. I don't even remember if we had any cookies with nuts in them in the case last week." Her words weren't meant for anyone but her, but when she felt Hunter's hand on her shoulder, she covered it with one of her own and let him offer comfort.

"Don't second-guess yourself. You didn't sell him anything," he said sympathetically.

"It's my word against his, and the customer is always right, right? What if I did sell that man a cookie with nuts and just don't remember? I could be in trouble."

"We'll cross that bridge if we get to it, and I highly doubt we will. Forget about it and focus on the Sweet Sounds fund-raiser tomorrow. And our dance."

Hunter's charm and concern mixed to give Jillian's mood a much-needed boost, but all the compassion in the world couldn't loosen the raw tension clenching her shoulders. As if she didn't have enough to worry about. Was she right and it was simply a misunderstanding? Or could she possibly have put that man's life in danger?

Jillian placed a Georgia peach pie on the long table filled to bursting with desserts. At the start of the fruit's season, it added a nice local touch to the Sweet Sounds fund-raiser. No matter how fancy the guests were in their finest fashions, there was always a place for a peach pie at a Southern event.

And this was certainly a grand affair. Held in the opulent main hall of the enormous mansion at Jardin d'Amandes, the event bustled with ladies in sequined and satin gowns and gentlemen wearing tails. Everyone held sparkling glasses delivered by the white-gloved waitstaff, and many carried cocktail plates laden with selections from Jillian's dessert table. The crowd had been dancing all evening to music provided by ensembles from the local high school as well as the professional pianist. Currently, a brass quintet was standing on the grand staircase, blasting away at "Basin Street Blues." Jillian thought they sounded a lot better than most high school musicians she'd heard in her day, and she felt a swell of local pride.

"How long are y'all going to make me wait to taste that peach pie? It looks mighty tasty."

Jillian glanced over her shoulder to find the tuxedo-clad piano player eyeing the dessert table. "Just the pie? Are you sure you don't want to try a mini crème brûlée? Or how about a raspberry scone?"

The handsome man grinned, popping out a single dimple that gave him a boyish appearance even though he had to be in his thirties. "Keep tempting me, and I may not fit behind the keyboard much longer." He gestured to a couple in their golden years who walked by, the silver-haired wife displaying a bedazzling choker of diamonds and rubies. "I believe the high school jazz band will do well by this crowd tonight. Don't you think?"

Jillian had to agree. The socialites in attendance were Moss Hollow's wealthiest set. "They shouldn't have any problem raising the funds for their trip to the national competition or the new uniforms and instruments to make them outshine their competitors."

"The kids deserve it," he said. "I'm glad to see Moss Hollow take care of their youth."

"Are you from around here?"

"Depends on your definition, I suppose. I have some ties to the community, though I make my home about an hour from here. Home is where you make it, isn't it?"

Jillian cut him the first piece of pie, finding that she liked this man. "Here, take this to the piano, and I promise to keep the sweets coming all night. Thank you for being a part of this fund-raiser, Mister . . ."

"Jeremiah Davis, ma'am. And much obliged." He took the plate she offered and retreated back toward a glossy black grand piano, pausing to compliment each guest he passed. His silky brown hair was thinning a bit at the forehead but Jillian could tell that the dimple in his left cheek made every lady he met ignore his receding hairline.

Jillian bit back a smile and watched Jeremiah move through the crowd like silk. He waited off to the side while the brass quintet wrapped up their song and left the steps, then approached the piano. When he reached his instrument, he pushed back his coattails with a flourish and took his seat at the keys. Then he began to play, and the room fell into an awed hush.

Hunter had been correct about the man's skills.

Jillian had to force herself to get back to her work. She lifted her large knife again to slice the rest of the pie into slivers. The peaches were caramelized to perfection in a glistening glaze thanks to the Southern Sweetie Pies and their skills the other night. She sent a silent prayer of thanks for her helpful friends. They had made all the difference in believing she could handle this catering event solo.

"Penny for your thoughts?"

Jillian startled from her daydreaming to find Hunter beside her, dashing in his formal wear. "Wow. You look . . ."

"Like a penguin who escaped from the zoo?" He offered her one of his disarming smiles, wiggling his eyebrows and pulling on the ends of his bow tie.

"Do you have to be back in your habitat by midnight?" she asked with a chuckle.

"Nope. I am a wild and free bird." Hunter grinned and reached for the large knife in her hand. "Here, let me cut these pies for you."

Jillian could handle cutting the pies, but the gesture was sweet, so she handed over the knife to let him help. She watched the guests twirl across the floor. "A successful evening, wouldn't you say?"

The music picked up, and she missed Hunter's reply. She took the nod of his head as his agreement. A beautiful mezzo-soprano voice lifted to the cathedral ceiling of the hall and drew the dancers' attention to the piano. A blonde woman had appeared near Jeremiah.

"Who's that?" someone asked nearby. Jillian didn't recognize the young lady either, so she waited for someone else to reply.

Hunter wiped the knife blade against a cloth napkin and set it on the table, then glanced toward the singer. He leaned close to Jillian and whispered, "That's Flannery Garland. Local celebrity and one-time Miss Georgia, I believe. Great voice, huh? I imagine she nailed the talent competition."

Jillian imagined the same. The pianist's smooth fingers flowed across the keys, and his accompanying vocalist was stunning, both in talent and beauty. Coiffed in an elegant twist, her golden hair glimmered in the candlelight that lit the grand hall. Her flawless face remained serene even as the notes she sang progressed to octaves most would never attempt. Even from across the room, Jillian could tell that Flannery's charmeuse gown was the same shade of cerulean as her eyes.

Jillian glanced down at her own attire—a standard server's outfit of black skirt and white shirt with a Chocolate Shoppe Bakery apron over it—and suddenly realized she'd taken several steps forward and melded with the crowd of spectators as though she was one of them. On a quick turn, she made her way back toward her table.

"Don't go far. I still want that dance." Hunter's voice followed her as she hustled to replenish her spread.

The song ended and was met by thunderous applause and loud cheers. "Encore! Encore!"

"First, a toast." A voice boomed through the room, and everyone turned to see an older gentleman standing on the curved staircase, an elegant elderly woman beside him. Jillian recognized her as Lucinda Atwood, the woman of the house and the chairwoman of the arts commission. She had given Jillian approximately thirty seconds of her time earlier in the day to verify that she was prepared for her duties that night. The no-nonsense woman seemed to prize efficiency and order.

Lucinda held firmly to the banister of the spiral staircase as she took another step down. Her dress appeared heavily laden with sparkling rhinestones and she wore a display window's worth of jewelry, but she held her head high. The candlelight cast a gleam on her glossy platinum locks, cut in a bob that curved out at her jawline.

The man, similar in age to Lucinda, continued. "A toast to my longtime friend and our gracious hostess, Lucinda Atwood.

This generous woman organized tonight's splendid event for you all, and for the good of our very own Moss Hollow High School jazz band. The evening is young, so there is plenty of time to be just as generous with your checkbooks as Lucinda has been with her home and her time as our arts commission's chairwoman."

Lucinda patted the man's arm affectionately with her bejeweled fingers and beamed admiration at him. She lifted a hand toward the piano and gave her own announcement. "And please, give a round of applause for our talented performers. I could hear their beautiful music from upstairs. Thank you, Mr. Jeremiah Davis. My late husband would have loved hearing you play. And thank you too, my dear, dear Flannery." Lucinda glanced at the man beside her. "You and your father, Earle, are everything to me. I would do just about anything for you both." She raised her arm higher in a grand sweeping gesture. "Let us continue with another song."

"Hear, hear!" someone in the crowd cheered, followed by a chorus of agreement.

Jeremiah's fingers hit the keys in a flourish, setting the next song in motion. Apparently caught off guard, Flannery gave the piano player a startled glance, but didn't miss her cue to come in. If the two hadn't practiced their encore, no one was the wiser. Flannery's voice rang out clear as a bell, a perfect companion to Jeremiah's lively piano playing. The crowd returned to their dancing and socializing, letting the music carry them away. Nobody saw the man clad in a blue button-down shirt and jeans step up behind the performers.

Suddenly, the man reached out and slammed the piano key cover down directly on Jeremiah's flying fingers. The clang echoed in the foyer as did Jeremiah's cry of pain. The piano player threw himself off the seat in an abrupt turn, his fists raised toward his assailant.

Jillian inhaled when she saw the men face off, but not because of the threat of violence. She recognized the newcomer's glaring face. It was the same man who had come into the bakery the day before claiming he would sue her. Was this another scheme? Or was there something else at play here?

"Sterling, no!" Flannery launched herself at the men, her hands stretched out toward the intruder. "You shouldn't be here. You need to leave right now."

"Why? So you can go back to cavorting with this leech?" The man surveyed the cavernous hall full of well-heeled socialites then announced, "Everybody, check your wallets. Jeremiah Davis is a thief."

At first, everyone stood still, stunned at the scene before them. Then, whispers and murmurs began to rumble through the crowd, and the rustling of fabric grew louder as partygoers searched their purses and coat pockets.

Jillian couldn't allow this blond intruder to ruin the event, not when it was fairly likely that he had nefarious intentions beyond rescuing the pageant queen from an alleged thief. If he'd come to Moss Hollow to cause trouble, everyone should know. She took several steps toward the staircase and raised her voice. "Jeremiah Davis has done nothing but entertain the good people of Moss Hollow. That's more than I can say for you—Sterling, is it?" she asked.

The man glanced her way. Confusion switched to recognition in the blink of an eye. His mouth twisted into a sinister smile. "The bakery lady. Tried to kill anybody else this week?"

Jillian moved to step forward again, but something pulled her back. Hunter's hand grasped her elbow. "Let him be, Jillian," he said under his breath. "Not worth it."

"Sterling, let's go." Flannery grabbed hold of the intruder's arm and pulled. Despite her increasingly desperate tugging, the man didn't budge. Pure hatred swathed his face, and it radiated

Jillian's way as he swept his malevolent stare over the crowd. He shook free of Flannery, his strength shoving her backward. The pageant beauty let out a scream before she landed hard on her side against the marbled tile floor, crumpled in a heap of silky fabric.

"How dare you!" Jeremiah lunged, hands in fists. Before he could land a punch, Sterling grabbed the pianist's lapels and shoved him back against a sculpted bust resting serenely on a white pedestal. The head toppled over and shattered. The men, too focused on annihilating each other, barely seemed to notice.

Jeremiah tackled Sterling, and they skidded across the shiny marble. Aside from the thud of their bodies hitting the ground and their ongoing wrestling match, the only sound was Flannery's shrieking as she scrambled to her feet.

"I'm leaving, Sterling Macon," Flannery shouted. "And I will never forgive you for this. You promised me you had changed. We're through!" She stormed out the side door, the glass door banging closed as Flannery stomped down the walkway to the walled gardens. Jillian saw her fair head bob above the tall hedges beyond, then disappear.

Jeremiah had pinned Sterling, but with a grunt, the blond man threw off the pianist and gained his feet. Jeremiah struggled to his knees, where he rested with his hands braced on his knees in an apparent effort to catch his breath.

Sterling swiped a trail of blood from his chin and spat so loud it echoed through the hall. "This isn't over," he growled. "I am sick of you showing up and ruining everything." Without warning, Sterling kicked Jeremiah in the stomach and took off after Flannery.

Jeremiah doubled over in a fit of coughing and groaning. He paused to recover. Then with a roar, he ran for the exit, apparently not finished with Sterling Macon just yet.

Having been frozen in place by shock at the display of violence, so incongruous for the elegant surroundings, Jillian shook her head to clear it. Everyone else in the room also seemed to be coming to their senses as well, and quiet murmuring grew quickly into animated chatter.

Jillian pivoted toward the stairs, where Lucinda still stood with Earle Garland. Jillian had thought the hostess might offer some direction, but the older woman's gray pallor didn't offer hope of receiving any. Hunter quietly slipped from Jillian's side and went out the French doors. Was he going after the men to stop any more fighting? She could always count on Hunter for his levelheadedness, though she wasn't sure it was wise to try to keep the peace between those two men.

With their hostess frozen in place on the staircase, Jillian realized the least she could do was distract the crowd. "Everyone, desserts are served," she announced over the din. "Why don't we replace all this bitterness with something sweet? And perhaps that wonderful quintet could come back and treat us to another song?"

Jillian's words seemed to snap the crowd out of their fixation on the ugly scene. The high school ensemble reassembled on the stairs and struck up a classic jazz number, then another. A line of guests gathered at the dessert table, and the plated offerings quickly disappeared. As Jillian was replenishing a platter of miniature pecan tarts, Lucinda appeared at her elbow.

"I'm sorry to hear you've had a run-in with that man," Lucinda said, a tremble in her voice. "I appreciate your efforts to help bring a little grace back to this affair."

"Not a problem, Mrs. Atwood. May I get you a piece of pie?"

"No, but did you happen to bring the scones I ordered?"

"They're right here." Jillian grabbed a plate and napkin.

"Cut one in half for me, would you, dear?"

"Of course." Jillian reached for the large knife she had been using to cut the pies, but her hand fell to an empty napkin.

Her knife was gone.

Then she remembered Hunter had taken it from her to finish cutting the pies. He must have put it down somewhere else. "Hold on one moment, Mrs. Atwood. I'll be right back."

After scooping a scone onto the plate in her hand, Jillian made her way to the kitchen. She found a clean knife in the butcher block and cut the scone down the middle. As the knife sliced through the perfectly crystalized glaze, Jillian caught a hint of almond extract wafting through the air. She smiled wryly. *Well, if nothing else goes right this evening, at least the food is tasty.*

She brought the knife to the sink to wash it. Just as she swiped it with the sponge, a bloodcurdling scream cut through the night air from outside the kitchen's exterior door.

Jillian jumped at the sound and jerked the blade into her finger. Crimson blood mixed with the stream of water raining from the faucet, and she hissed as pain overtook her. All she could do was grab a towel and press it to her hand to staunch the flow.

With the towel wrapped around her finger, Jillian ran to the door that led out into the gardens. As she stepped over the threshold, she saw who had screamed. And then she saw why.

Sterling Macon lay facedown in the tulips, a knife protruding from his back.

"He's dead!" A frantic Flannery was kneeling beside him, cradling his lifeless head in the blue silk covering her lap. "My Sterling is dead!"

People cascaded down the path from the hall, gaping first at Flannery, and then at Jillian on the nearby step. They continued to gaze at Jillian, confused expressions marring their faces.

Jillian pushed a red curl that had escaped her hairnet away from her face. More eyes widened in concern. *Why are they looking at me like that?*

"Jillian?" Hunter walked up the path from around the front of the house. He too searched her face.

"Hunter," she said, "Sterling Macon has been stabbed."

"I've been up and down on this property trying to find them and stop any violence. I wish I'd succeeded." He stared at her. "You have blood on your face and hands."

As Hunter pulled out his cell phone to call the police, Jillian reached for her cheek and noticed the bloody towel in her tight grasp, her knuckles blaring white. She lifted her injured hand. She must have touched her face and hadn't realized it.

"The knife," was all she could manage when he hung up.

Hunter hunched down beside Sterling's body. "It's yours. The swirling design matches the one I used to cut the pies. You cut yourself on it? I'm assuming that happened before it landed in his back."

"What?" She crouched beside him as if getting closer to him would help her understand his words. "No, I didn't cut myself on that knife." She glanced toward the door behind her. Beyond it was the knife that had cut her, resting in the sink.

"There's a second one?" Hunter's question pulled her attention back to him.

"I was cutting a scone." Her response felt lame and useless. "I heard a scream and came out here. I have no idea how my knife got . . . there. I hadn't seen it since you took it to cut the pie for me."

"I left it on the table," Hunter said. "Anyone could have picked it up."

As Hunter glanced at the growing crowd of onlookers spilling from the home, his words had many shaking their heads and backing away.

"No one is to leave these grounds," Hunter said loudly. "The police have been called and will have a copy of the attendance list. In the meantime, everyone please return to the hall to avoid contaminating the scene."

"What about her?" Jillian nodded to Flannery, who sobbed quietly.

Hunter approached Flannery and placed a hand on her shoulder. "Miss Garland."

She jerked at Hunter's touch. "We were going to be married," she said. "It was all going to be so perfect."

"I'm sorry, but I need you to come away from here. You could disturb evidence, and that will make it harder to find out who did this."

"I know who did it."

"You do?"

Flannery's head snapped up, eyes wide in fear. Her throat convulsed as she swallowed a few times.

"Can you tell me who you think killed Sterling?" Hunter's soothing voice seemed to soften Flannery's strained expression, but she didn't respond immediately.

Sirens blared in the distance. Flannery glanced toward the sound, her eyes dulled by shock. Her gaze moved to run over the crowd, as if she tried to examine each guest.

Jeremiah Davis appeared from behind the hedge closest to the kitchen door, winded as though he'd run some distance to get there.

His eyes alighted on Jillian. "I lost them," he said breathlessly, shaking his head. "Hopefully, that man doesn't hurt her. Again." Jeremiah glanced around at the crowd of partygoers who hadn't gone inside as instructed. "Flannery, you're here. Are you okay?" His gaze dropped to the man beside her. "What happened?"

"As if you don't know." Flannery glared at Jeremiah.

Spectators inhaled sharply. There was a killer among them, and they were all too happy to accept it wasn't one of Moss Hollow's socialites. One by one the crowd spoke up.

"The dead guy had something on the piano player," one man said.

"He said Davis was a crook," came an answer from the man's friend. "And my wallet is missing."

"Search him!" the first man commanded.

Jeremiah put his hands up, his face awash with panic. "I didn't do anything. I swear."

Lucinda stepped from the crowd with Earle Garland at her elbow. "I trusted you, Jeremiah. I gave you this opportunity to begin afresh. And this is how you repay me?" Her voice trembled. "How could you?"

Jillian could sense the pain radiating from the anguished expression on Jeremiah's face. The woman's words had apparently cut him deeper than any blade could.

In the next instant, police burst onto the scene in pairs, coming from every direction. Jillian caught sight of Deputy Laura Lee Zane, her work transforming her from a Southern Sweetie Pie into a uniformed woman on a mission. She was here to catch a killer.

Time seemed to move in slow motion from that point on. After cleaning the blood off herself and getting a bandage for her cut, Jillian loitered with the rest of the guests in the grand hall, where the police had gathered everyone. Hunter switched hats from partygoer to coroner and worked to process the scene and the body. Some officers questioned the guests while one kept an eye on Jeremiah Davis, who sat at the piano with his head in his hands.

Jillian wondered if they would take Jeremiah into custody. How could they when all they had was hearsay from guests who had been inside when Sterling's murder had occurred? She watched the piano player as he sat hunched on the bench, his back to the keys. She felt a strong pull to comfort him. *Don't be a fool*, she told herself. *The man is supposedly a thief.* She'd exchanged maybe half a dozen sentences with Jeremiah, but there was just something about him that struck her as innocent—of murder, anyway.

Laura Lee's voice pulled Jillian from her thoughts as the deputy arrived in the room and called out, "Mr. Alton Porter?"

"That's me." The older gentleman who had claimed his wallet had been taken stepped forward.

Laura Lee held up a wallet in her gloved hands. "Is this your wallet?"

The man squinted as he neared it. She had it open to his ID. "Why, yes it is. Where did you find it?"

"I found it in Jeremiah Davis's car."

Jeremiah raised his head when he heard his name. He stood up slowly, his grim face pinched in anger. "Something tells me I'm going with you." At her nod, his face hardened and he pushed his hands forward, wrists extending from the sleeves of his tuxedo jacket. "Let's get this over with."

"I see you know the drill," Laura Lee said, approaching Jeremiah. She took her handcuffs off her belt and opened them, then clicked them shut around the man's wrists. "Jeremiah Davis, you are under arrest."

As Laura Lee led the man away, Jillian could hear the fading explanation of why he was being taken into custody. He was a thief, just as Sterling Macon had said—moments before being murdered.

Jillian felt a heavy wave of exhaustion. She was long past ready to pack up her things and go home to Belle Haven. She made her way back to the kitchen, her footsteps leaden. As she passed one of the grand hall's marble pillars, she caught sight of Lucinda embracing a sobbing Flannery. Jillian was glad the young pageant queen had a shoulder to cry on at this difficult time. With a dead fiancé, she'd need all the help she could get.

The next morning, Jillian found Bertie and Cornelia sitting at the table in Belle Haven's cozy kitchen. The twin sisters were dressed in their Sunday best, Bertie in her usual reserved fashion and Cornelia in her usual outrageous fashion, which today included an oversize silk daisy pin on the lapel of a turquoise suit jacket and a matching pill hat perched on her head. Jillian thought she saw Bertie's lips purse with disapproval at the turquoise eye shadow her sister sported.

Bertie smoothed her simple taupe skirt as she greeted her granddaughter. "Good morning. Sleep well?"

"Like a rock. Have you eaten breakfast already?" Jillian asked.

Bertie nodded. "An hour ago. We let you sleep. You needed it after last night. We didn't keep anything for you because we didn't know when you'd be up."

"That's fine." Jillian opened the refrigerator door and peered in with indecision. She didn't feel hungry and nothing looked appetizing. She settled on a yogurt, then retrieved a spoon from the drawer and sat down with her family. She peeled back the lid and gave the yogurt a stir but abandoned the spoon with a dramatic sigh.

"You don't sound fine," Bertie said with her typical acuity. "Care to tell us what happened?"

"You know what happened. The whole town knows."

"It was a hot topic of conversation on the bus back from the retreat last night," Cornelia admitted. "One of the girls got a text about it from her neighbor, who was at the party. Of course, I already knew about it from my tear-out cards." Cornelia kept tear-out cards from magazines and claimed she could predict the future with them.

Bertie shot her sister a glare. "I still can't believe you brought those things on a church retreat. And you didn't know about any murder from them."

Cornelia sniffed haughtily. "I knew *something* was going to happen."

Bertie rolled her eyes and refocused her attention on Jillian. "I meant what happened to you? Your feathers are ruffled."

"What do you expect?" Jillian slumped in her chair. "I saw a dead man who had been murdered with my knife. That's not an everyday occurrence."

"The police don't think you did it, do they?"

"No. Well, I hope not. The knife was left out where anyone could have taken it."

"But did anyone else have a run-in with the victim?" Bertie asked. "You did, and everyone knows it."

"I didn't have a 'run-in.'" Jillian put air quotes around the words. "You make it sound like we had a sordid past."

"He claimed you nearly killed him last week. That's sordid enough to give you motive."

"But I *didn't*. I'd never met him before. Now, if it's all the same to you, I need to get ready for church." Jillian shoved back her chair and stood. She tossed the spoon in the sink and the uneaten yogurt in the trash as she headed for the stairs.

"Don't keep it bottled up, dear," Cornelia called from behind. "It will stifle your *joie de vivre.*"

Jillian stopped at the bottom of the stairs, but not because of Cornelia's warning. Possum trotted down the steps and met her shins with a loud meow of greeting. "What are you being so friendly for?" she demanded grumpily.

Cornelia gasped with a melodramatic flair and rushed to Jillian's side. "See? Even Raymond recognizes your angst. He's picking up on your vibes."

"No, *Possum* smells bacon and thinks I have it." Jillian couldn't find the patience to humor her great-aunt this morning.

"Right here, honey." Impervious to Jillian's attitude, Cornelia opened the microwave and pulled out a single strip of bacon, obviously with the cat's name on it.

"You made the cat breakfast, but you didn't save any for me?" Jillian said incredulously.

"Raymond isn't picky if his bacon is cold. You are." Cornelia broke the strip in two and held out half to Jillian. "Care to share?"

The cat meowed his disapproval.

Jillian laughed, her first burst of joviality since last night. She bent to stroke the cat's creamy fur, saving an extra scratch for his chocolate-colored ears. "Don't worry, Possum. I wouldn't dream of swiping your bacon."

Cornelia put Possum's treat on a plate and set it down in front of him.

Bertie stepped up to wrap an arm around Jillian. "Why do I get the feeling this glum face isn't just about your knife ending up in that man's back?"

Jillian shrugged and leaned into her grandmother's embrace, taking comfort in her familiar warmth and scent.

Cornelia clapped her hands. "I've got it. We'll haul that piano down from the attic and bring some music back into Belle Haven. That would liven up this dusty old place."

Bertie shook her head. "Can't you see Jillian needs some peace and quiet? Not some out-of-tune noise machine."

"Nonsense. A little music always makes me feel better."

Jillian frowned. "Cornelia, I appreciate the thought, but a piano is the last thing I want to see right now. I thought the piano player at the fund-raiser was such a great guy, so kind and friendly, and then it turned out he's probably a murderer. A thief at the very least."

"Don't be so hard on yourself, Jillian." Bertie gave her another strong squeeze and then released her. "You see the best in people. That's nothing to beat yourself up about."

"Besides," Cornelia chimed in, "if this Macon fella was as big a rat to anyone else as he was to you about a cookie you never served, maybe he got what was coming to him."

"Sister, suggesting that a man deserved to die with a chef's knife in his back is unbecoming to say the least," Bertie said sharply.

"Well if Jillian will hustle and get ready, we can all go to church." Cornelia adjusted her daisy pin. "I can ask God's forgiveness for my unbecoming habit of telling it like it is."

After service later that morning, Jillian, Bertie, and Cornelia descended the steps of Moss Hollow Fellowship Church amid other parishioners wearing summer-weight suits and colorful dresses. As they approached the parking lot, Jillian caught sight of Annalise Reed a few yards ahead. Annalise was wearing a lovely lilac-hued sheath dress, and her husband, Byron, was wearing a gray suit Jillian figured he wore often in his job as vice president at the bank. They were a charming couple, Jillian thought, then called out for her friend to wait up.

Annalise stopped near a magnolia tree and turned toward Jillian while Byron moved on toward their blue Volvo. "Hi, Jillian."

"I just wanted to thank you for your help the other night," Jillian said. "There's no way we could have done it without you."

"That's what friends are for," Annalise said, sounding rather distracted to Jillian's ears.

Bertie and Cornelia joined them under the tree as a car horn sounded. Everyone turned toward the Volvo, where Byron was standing with one foot inside the driver's door, motioning to his wife to hurry.

"Hold your horses, Byron," Bertie called. "We have Sweetie Pie business to take care of."

Byron shook his head and climbed behind the wheel of his car, slamming the door just a little too hard.

"Is everything all right, dear?" Cornelia asked. "Byron doesn't seem his normal genteel self. I daresay I've never heard him *honk* at you."

Annalise glanced her husband's way and twisted the strap of her white leather purse. "Everything's fine, really. Just some stress he's under at work. I'll be over to the meeting after lunch. But don't wait for me, okay?"

"Sure thing, sweetie." Bertie's tone sounded very much as though she wasn't buying it.

After Annalise hurried to the Volvo, they watched Byron speed out of the church parking lot. "Something's up with that pair," Cornelia said. "Trouble in paradise."

Jillian shook her head. "I'm sure everything is fine. Let's wait to see what Annalise wants to share before jumping to conclusions."

"Jillian's right," Bertie said. "No sense in speculating now. The truth always comes out in the end."

"Well, aren't you all a merry bunch? Did someone die or something?" Lenora elbowed Jillian with a plump arm as she joined them by the tree. "Whoops, sorry, Jillian. I wasn't thinking. That was a horrible thing to say, given what you had to deal with last night."

"Is there anybody in town who doesn't know what happened at Jardin d'Amandes last night?" Jillian sighed, then saw Hunter step out of the church. He scanned the front lawn until his eyes fell on her. As their gazes met, she smiled reflexively, but he didn't respond in kind.

He took the steps slowly, stopping at the foot of the stairs. His pause stumped her, but it was his frown that worried her. By the time he reached her under the shade of the magnolia tree, her smile was long gone.

"Something wrong?" she asked with growing nervousness.

"Yes. We need to talk." Hunter nodded hello to Bertie, Cornelia, and Lenora, then guided Jillian a few feet away from the tree.

"What's up?" The upbeat squeak in her voice was unconvincing.

Hunter reached inside his suit coat's breast pocket. He pulled out a piece of paper, which she saw quickly was a photo. As he brought it near, she saw it was a picture of The Chocolate Shoppe Bakery's storefront. Upon closer inspection, she saw that she herself was at the window in the picture.

"Where did this come from?" she asked, taking the image into her hand to study it. In it, her arms were crossed and her face was set in a scornful way. It certainly wasn't the most flattering picture she'd ever taken.

"It was on Sterling Macon's cell phone, and he posted it on his social media page with an angry message," Hunter said. "He must have snapped it the day he barged in."

"I forgot he took this. What does it mean?"

Hunter remained serious. "It could mean nothing. But it could mean the sheriff will come calling to find out more about your involvement with Macon."

"I have no involvement. He was a liar. I never sold him anything." She thrust the picture back at Hunter as though it burned her.

Hunter returned the photo to his pocket as Bertie stepped up to them. "We're heading home for lunch, then to the Sweetie Pies meeting. Are you coming?"

The Southern Sweetie Pies met every Sunday at the bakery, chatting about recipes and goings-on about town. Jillian usually loved every minute of it, but she wasn't sure she was in the mood for company. "I think I'll just stay home today, Bertie."

"Stay home? What's gotten into you, child?" Bertie glanced Hunter's way, her keen eyes flashing concern. "Does this have something to do with what happened last night?"

Hunter nodded. "I thought Jillian should know the police will probably want to talk to her about a photo."

"What photo?" Bertie's eyes narrowed.

"One of her, taken by the deceased," Hunter said. "He had posted it on his social media page with a few—shall we say—choice words about the bakery."

"Well, that's absurd. Jillian didn't do anything to that man." Bertie faced Jillian. "And if the police want to talk to you today, they can find you at the bakery. That's where you'll be, surrounded by your friends and family. Now, come on and get in the car. Cornelia is waiting."

Hunter's lips quirked up at the corners. "You heard her, Jillian. Get in the car." He briefly took her hand, giving it a squeeze of reassurance.

Despite her affection for Hunter, Jillian didn't feel particularly reassured. Instead, she felt as though Sterling Macon was reaching out from beyond the grave to make her life as difficult as possible.

5

Rising early Monday morning after a fitful night of sleep, Jillian arrived at the bakery before Bertie, and even before Lenora came down from the upstairs apartment. She was soon immersed in work. She opened the oven door and peeked at a batch of scones, then decided they could use a few more minutes. She returned to the large worktable, where several trays of lemon muffins waited to be drizzled with icing.

The repetitive work let Jillian's mind work on another task: trying to figure out who Sterling Macon really was, and what his plans for her had been.

Now that she'd thought about it for a few days, she was certain she had never served Sterling Macon a cookie with nuts in it, or indeed, any kind of cookie—which made her even more uneasy about the fact that he'd acted so certain that it was her, specifically, who had sold it to him. That was strange enough, but why had he felt the need to take her photo? And not only that, but to post the photo all over social media as well? He seemed to have been set on causing trouble at any cost, even if he was wrong.

A knock on the back door startled Jillian out of her thoughts, and she dropped her piping bag on top of the muffin she was decorating. With a groan of frustration, Jillian moved the bag aside, then pulled off her plastic gloves and walked toward the door. Before she got there, a harder knock sounded.

"Jillian? Are you in there? It's Deputy Jones. I need to ask you a few questions."

"Gooder?"

Goodman "Gooder" Jones was one of the deputies with the

Nathan County sheriff's office. They'd gone to high school together, which was where he'd earned his nickname. Jillian had helped him solve several cases since moving back to town, though he didn't always appreciate her assistance.

Jillian opened the back door to find Gooder's somber face. *This must be an official call.* "Trying to beat the crowd for your morning coffee?" Her jovial attitude fell as flat as a ruined soufflé.

"Anybody else around? I was hoping to speak to you before it gets, ah, too crowded in here."

"Bertie won't be here for fifteen or twenty minutes, and Lenora hasn't come down yet." Jillian let Gooder inside and closed the door after him. "Hunter told me to be expecting you."

"I reckon he did." Gooder removed his brimmed officer's hat and rubbed a hand across his close-cropped dark hair. His green eyes followed her as she returned to her task of dripping glaze on muffins. "Jillian, tell me this: Why is it that every time we have a dead body, you're always close at hand? Scratch that. Instead, tell me why I'm still surprised to hear about it."

"I've never been able to figure out how you think."

"Would you like to answer my questions seriously?"

"Why start now?"

Gooder frowned. "Jillian, this may come as a surprise, but I'm not here to fight with you. I'm just trying to do my job. As you said, you know why I'm here."

Jillian sighed and leaned against the worktable. "I know. I'm sorry. Go ahead and ask me what you want. And have a muffin while you're at it. You're awfully crabby when you're hungry." She gestured to the tray. "In answer to your question about why I'm always around, I really can't answer that for you. Aunt Cornelia would probably tell you I'm supernaturally drawn to that kind of thing. You know how she is. But in this particular situation, I was there for a legitimate reason, since I was catering the event."

Gooder studied her briefly, his expression unreadable, then grabbed the closest muffin. He took a bite, and Jillian thought he almost smiled at the taste. Recovering himself, he swallowed, then pulled out a notebook and flipped it to a blank page, pencil at the ready. "I understand you had a confrontation with Sterling Macon a few days before he was killed. He was threatening to ruin the bakery, accusing you of nearly killing him."

"At one time, I might have said he had a case, but not anymore," Jillian said drily. "You have to admit, my baking has gotten a lot better."

One of Gooder's eyebrows shot up, but he didn't respond to her comment. Instead, he asked, "Did you sell him a food product he was allergic to?"

"No, I did not. And none of the other employees did either. I asked. Actually, I don't remember him ever setting foot in this bakery until he showed up threatening me. I think he was looking for fast cash. He probably figured that if he could get me all flustered, I would throw money at him to make the threat go away, whether I was guilty or not. Which I'm not. Of any of it. Selling him a cookie with nuts, or sinking a knife into his back."

"Jillian, there's no need to get defensive. No more than usual, anyway." Gooder cleared his throat. "Now, I have to ask you where you were when his body was found."

"Didn't I already tell you guys this on Saturday night?"

"Please just answer the question. I need to put together a detailed account of everyone's whereabouts."

"Every suspect's whereabouts, you mean. How many other folks are you interviewing twice?"

"Would you just answer the question, Jillian?" he snapped.

Her shoulders slumped. "Fine. I was in the Jardin d'Amandes kitchen cleaning a knife, which I had just cut my finger on. As previously stated and proven with your handy little swab test, it was my own blood on my hands, not Sterling Macon's. Anyway,

I heard Flannery scream and ran out the kitchen door to find her kneeling over his body with his head in her lap."

"The kitchen door. So you had your own way in and out to the garden, where Sterling Macon was found."

"Yes." Jillian felt the walls closing in around her. Gooder sounded as though he was trying to make more of this than it was.

"And he was found a few yards from this door."

"Yes."

"Stabbed by your knife."

"Yes."

"Was there a view from this vantage point to the inside hall where the guests were gathered?"

"No. There was a large hedge around the path that gave privacy to the garden from the hall."

"So, no one would have seen you step out or back into the kitchen through the private entrance?"

Jillian crossed her arms at her chest. "I don't like your implications, Deputy."

Gooder closed the cover of the pad in one flip and pushed the pencil through the rings at the top. "Nobody likes a murderer on the loose. I'm just trying to do my job to be sure our bases are covered."

"A murderer on the loose? I thought you arrested Jeremiah Davis for the murder."

"Davis is being detained on theft charges. That's everything we have evidence for right now, and he's not confessing to anything."

"He's not confessing to stealing that wallet found in his car? So if he's a thief, then he's also a liar."

"Well, someone is a liar, that's for sure." Gooder's pointed look silenced Jillian abruptly.

Footsteps on the back stairs announced Lenora arriving for her shift. "Good morning," she said, her gaze jumping skeptically from Jillian to Gooder and back again. "Hello, Gooder. I wasn't expecting to see you here so early. Couldn't wait for breakfast?"

"Just testing the merchandise." He shrugged and took another bite of muffin. "Not bad."

"Not bad?" Lenora laughed. "That almost sounded like a compliment to me. Are you going soft or something?"

"Not if I can help it. Now, if you'll excuse me, ladies, I have an investigation to get back to." After replacing his hat on his head, he stepped out the back door and let it close with a soft click.

"What was that all about?" Lenora asked as she brought a pink hairnet over her thick black hair.

Jillian scoffed and returned to her muffins. "Sometimes I just don't know what Gooder is up to."

Lenora tied her apron around her robust middle, and her eyes turned thoughtful. "Honey, you aren't thinking Gooder really believes you could be guilty of murdering that fellow?"

"He has me on the list, but I'm just happy he's looking beyond Jeremiah Davis. If it's not him—and it's definitely not me—then there's a murderer running around Moss Hollow. The sooner Gooder catches whoever actually did it, the better."

Lenora pulled the oven door wide. Black smoke billowed out at them, filling the kitchen with a burnt haze. "Mercy, girl."

"The scones! I forgot about them with Gooder here." Jillian raced for the oven mitts. "They're all burned."

"I'd say so." Lenora opened the back door to let the smoke out. "Good thing Bertie hasn't arrived yet. She'd think you were reverting back to your old days and ruining the inventory."

"Hopefully we can get the smoke cleared out before she gets here. Let's just keep this between us, shall we?"

"Sure thing, but you better figure out who Jeremiah Davis is and his connection to Sterling Macon. If they were working together, there's a good chance you could get burned too."

"'Beauty Queen's Fiancé Stabbed With Baker's Knife at Fund-Raiser.'" Savannah's voice was a little loud for Jillian's taste as she read the newspaper headline aloud in the bakery's seating area.

"Could you keep it down? I'd like to keep the customers we still have, thank you very much." Jillian continued scrubbing bistro tables with a little more force than was strictly necessary. "And what if James ended up dead somewhere? How would you like it if the newspaper headline was 'Accountant's Fiancé Chokes on Tax Return' or some such nonsense?"

"Cheer up," Savannah said. "They say there's no such thing as bad publicity. And judging by how busy you said it was today, people aren't staying away."

Jillian wiped down the last bistro table and tossed her cloth in the bucket of soapy water. She checked to see if Maggie had the last of the day's customers taken care of and then untied her apron. She slung it over the back of the chair across from Savannah, then dropped onto the seat with a sigh.

"Check this out." Savannah flattened the newspaper on the table, the engagement ring on her finger flashing in the late afternoon sun streaming through the window. "It says here that Sterling Macon has no known relatives. I find that interesting. Flannery Garland doesn't strike me as the type to marry someone who couldn't elevate her status."

"What are you saying?"

Savannah shrugged. "Only that I wouldn't jump to conclusions that Jeremiah Davis is the one to blame for the murder simply because he was the only accused criminal at the fund-raiser. The police haven't made an arrest for murder yet. If they had evidence, they would have already, don't you think? And they definitely wouldn't be coming after you. I think Gooder was fishing."

"Yes, but Jeremiah could be just as easily guilty as not guilty."

Savannah tilted her head. "I mean, if he's guilty that'll keep Gooder from knocking on your door at the crack of dawn again. We should write down what we know." Savannah tapped a finger against her chin. Some idea was percolating in her brain, Jillian was sure of it. "I need a pen."

Jillian grabbed one from the register. "What are you thinking?"

Savannah scribbled on the newspaper. Jillian tried to read it, but from her vantage point the writing was upside down and Savannah's hand moved too fast. Finally, Jillian could make out some sort of diagram.

"A family tree?" Jillian guessed.

"Of sorts, yes. The two men knew each other, right?"

"Yes, Sterling hinted that he had something on Jeremiah. They definitely knew each other."

"Yes, but as friend or foe? I've made two sides to this diagram. One side is for details on Sterling Macon. The other side is for Jeremiah Davis. What we need to do is some digging to find out how their lives are connected."

"The one person I'm sure knew both of them is Flannery Garland. She sang with Jeremiah, and apparently, she was going to marry Sterling."

"That's a good start," Savannah said. "And didn't you say that Jeremiah followed her out of the hall, and she was discovered with the body?"

Jillian nodded. "But I doubt she's the one who killed him. She'd have to be a pretty amazing actress if her hysteria wasn't authentic."

Savannah doodled in one of the margins. "So who else at the party could have been connected to both men?"

Faces spun through Jillian's memory. She recalled Lucinda

Atwood regally descending the curving staircase, then shook her head at the absurdity. Lucinda had needed help down those steps—she wouldn't have been able to chase Sterling down and sink a knife into his back. Besides, she'd been asking for a scone right about the time the man would have been killed.

Jillian grabbed the pen from Savannah's hand. She made a line between Jeremiah's name and Sterling's. "I'm convinced Sterling Macon was trying to pull a con on me. And Jeremiah was apparently a thief. They found that wallet in his car, and he seemed to know the drill when he was arrested. Two criminals in the same place at the same time? Sounds to me like they could have been working together. You know what they say: Birds of a feather stick together."

"Flock. It's 'Birds of a feather flock together.'"

"Whatever."

Savannah smirked. "So then, assuming your hypothesis is correct and they were working together, what happened to pit them against each other?"

Jillian tapped the pen by Jeremiah's name. She quickly circled his name and dropped the pen to the table, her mind made up.

She lowered her voice so Bertie wouldn't hear her plan. The woman was probably listening to every word through the swinging door. "I think my search starts with a trip to the county jail to pay Jeremiah a visit. There's a story there, and it's time to find out what it is."

6

"Drop your keys and purse in the tray," a female guard instructed Jillian at the county jail. Jillian did as she was told. The guard stepped away and pushed a code into a box next to the big steel door that separated the security checkpoint from the visiting chamber. A loud beep echoed through the concrete-walled space as the door unlocked.

Jillian followed the guard through the door. As soon as the door slammed behind her, she heard it lock again. They entered a dingy, windowless room that had two folding chairs positioned in front of a scratched and smeared glass. A phone receiver attached to a partition was the only other item in the room.

Through the glass, Jillian saw a mirror image of the room she stood in, although the door on that side stood open. Jeremiah Davis appeared in the doorway, handcuffs encircling his wrists.

Jillian's guard stepped to the wall and clasped her hands at her front, her face stoic. *I guess her part is done*, Jillian thought.

The male guard on the prisoners' side removed Jeremiah's handcuffs, then moved to the wall. The pianist slowly came to his chair, his eyes squinting at Jillian through the glass. He sat and waited for Jillian.

Jillian inhaled deeply, blanching at the room's stale odor, and then took her seat. She and Jeremiah stared at each other, not speaking. At first glance, she'd been reminded of the charming, kind man she had chatted with briefly at the fund-raiser. But the longer she gazed at him, the more she noticed how the harsh fluorescent lighting and cinder-block walls washed him out. His angular cheekbones made his eyes look rather sunken, and he appeared at once tired and on edge.

She dropped her attention to his bright orange jumpsuit, then down to his hands, now folded in front of him. His long fingers twisted around each other in an anxious grip.

Jillian picked up the phone receiver on the wall and gestured for him to do the same. After a short hesitation, he grasped the receiver and put it to his ear, but he didn't speak.

"Do you know who I am?" Jillian asked.

He nodded once. "I never forget a face. You're the baker." His voice rumbled deep and smooth through the phone.

"That's right. I . . ." She faltered, then cleared her throat to try again.

"I'm sorry I never got around to eating my pie," he said before she found her words. "It promised to be mighty delicious."

"I suppose they don't serve pie in jail, do they?" Jillian felt an instant wave of embarrassment. What was she saying? She'd never get any information out of Jeremiah if she kept acting like a fool. And the sooner she could get him talking, the sooner she could leave this awful place and go home to Belle Haven where she belonged.

But Jeremiah gave her a small grin. "No. And if they did, I doubt it would be as good as yours. How may I be of service to you today?"

Jillian bit the inside of her cheek, willing herself to get it together. "Did you know Sterling Macon came into my bakery to accuse me of selling him a cookie with nuts that nearly killed him?"

A smirk curled Jeremiah's lips as he shook his head in disbelief. "That old trick? It was a scam. You didn't sell him anything."

"I know I didn't, but how do *you* know that?"

"Because I know Sterling well. Or knew him anyway."

"Were you actually working with him? Before he cut you out of the deal?"

Jeremiah's sharp eyebrows shot up at her accusation. "What do you want, lady?"

"I'm wondering if maybe Sterling Macon double-crossed you. Something like that could make somebody pretty mad. Mad enough to kill, even."

Jeremiah's expression darkened and his body tensed visibly. He looked ready to spring at her. Jillian suddenly feared for her safety as though no partition existed. The ticking of the clock on the wall seemed to ricochet in Jillian's head during the long seconds of silence between her and the prisoner behind the glass. She'd point-blank accused him of murder, and she had no way of knowing what the fallout would be.

"Who are you working for?" Jeremiah's usually melodic voice had turned guttural.

She gaped at him in confusion. "Excuse me? I worked for Lucinda Atwood the night of the fund-raiser, if that's what you mean."

"No, I mean who put you up to coming here? You're trying to get me to confess." He leaned close to the glass, snarling. "How much are they paying you?"

"No one put me up to anything. I—I came here all on my own." Her bravado faltered as she spoke.

Anger scorched Jeremiah's face and his nostrils flared with rage.

Jillian recoiled. Coming here had been a mistake. What had she been thinking, confronting a suspected killer? Had she really thought he would confess to her when the police had had no such luck?

In an instant, Jeremiah's face softened and he leaned back in his chair. "So, maybe it was you who set me up, then." He ran his gaze over her, shaking his head as though he couldn't believe what he saw. "I wouldn't have believed it, but then, that's what makes a good con." He snorted derisively. "Imagine that, the baker did it. Did you hear that, guard? The real killer could be sitting right here." He returned his sneer to Jillian. "Did you plant the wallet too?"

"I didn't kill that man." Jillian's words spilled out involuntarily. Was he trying to turn the tables on her? Get her to confess to something she hadn't done? She realized in an instant that maybe that was exactly what she'd been doing to him, and she felt an icy trickle of shame along her spine.

"Well, let's see about that." He lifted his free hand with one finger pointed up. "First off, the knife belonged to you. And two—" his next finger shot up "—you had closer access to the garden than anyone. Brilliant, really. Get rid of the man who was pulling a scam on you, and then blame it on me."

"That's not true. I—" She stopped herself. "How do you know the kitchen had access to the garden? Did you case the joint before you started lifting wallets?"

"Get out of here." His nostrils flared and he jumped up. "Guard! Get this woman out of here. She's trying to trick me into confessing."

The guard stepped forward behind Jeremiah and grasped his arm. Jillian realized her own guard now stood beside her.

"This visit is over," the guard said to her. "Time to go, ma'am."

Jillian stood, but before she hung up the phone, Jeremiah spoke one last time.

Gone was the sweet-talking charmer from the fund-raiser. "You're going to regret this. You're going to regret coming here." He threw his receiver at the glass with such a force that Jillian dropped her own and shrank back toward her guard, arms raised in front of her face defensively.

A peek over her forearm showed Jeremiah being hauled away by his guard while he dragged his feet, his vicious gaze locked on her.

Jillian couldn't handle another second in this jail. After rushing back through the security checkpoint, she burst through the doors she had entered through and didn't stop until she stood across the street beside a lamppost. Leaning against the black metal, Jillian clutched her stomach and willed her racing heart to calm down.

The jail loomed ahead of her, its sharp edges creating menacing shadows in the waning daylight. Images of what had just happened flashed relentlessly through her mind: the way Jeremiah's fingers gripped the phone, the tense hunch of his shoulders, the heat and anger flaring in his eyes.

But there was something else in his gaze. What was it?

Jillian slowly straightened. "No, I don't believe it," she said aloud to herself. "He did it. He must have."

Except his eyes . . .

Had she seen something other than rage in them? Had she seen despair and distrust?

She studied the jail. Its solid exterior was impenetrable, its heavy doors made to protect the world from its inhabitants. But what if they also protected an inhabitant from someone outside its walls?

Jeremiah had sounded quite sure someone was paying her to set him up. But who? And why?

Jillian made her way to her Prius. She climbed in behind the wheel with a growing numbness. Out of the fog came a question that grew in strength until it was practically splashed across her mind's eye in neon paint.

What if Sterling hadn't been in town just to swindle a local bakery? What if Jeremiah had been Sterling's real mark?

Bright and early Tuesday morning, Jillian was just drizzling icing onto a batch of raspberry scones—unburnt this time—when the door between the kitchen and the front of the bakery swung open.

Maggie popped her head into the kitchen. "I'm opening for the day," she announced. "We've already got a customer, although I suspect he's not here for the bear claws." She winked at Jillian.

Jillian peered through the door Maggie held wide to see the one person outside the storefront window. She smiled and gave Hunter a wave.

He scowled in return.

Jillian couldn't fathom a reason for his irritation. "He looks crabby. Let the man in and get him some coffee, would you please?"

"I'm on it."

The door swung closed, but not for long. Hunter burst through it like a derailed locomotive.

"What on earth are you doing?" Jillian demanded.

"I should be asking you that." He seemed mad enough that she was surprised not to see steam blasting from his ears. He hadn't even combed his hair yet that morning, or if he had, he'd run through a wind tunnel on the way over.

"What are you talking about?" Jillian glanced over her shoulder at Bertie and Lenora, who had been hard at work on the other side of the kitchen but were currently standing straight up like prairie dogs in a meadow.

"Let's take this outside, shall we?" Jillian quickly grasped Hunter's arm and pulled him out the back door, letting it slam shut behind them. She'd never seen him quite this disheveled, and she was one hundred percent sure it was because he'd heard about her visit to the county jail the night before. "I don't understand why you're so upset. It's perfectly safe to visit people at the jail. There's a glass wall and guards."

Hunter swept an aggravated hand through his hair, making it stick out even more. "Safe? *Safe?* I can't believe what I'm hearing." He took a deep breath and began again. "That man is suspected of stabbing someone in the back. Why would you go there?"

Her defense stuck to the roof of her mouth. She had every right, but something on Hunter's face stopped her. He was genuinely worried for her, even scared.

She loosened her grip on his arm and opted for the peacemaker's approach. "I'm okay, Hunter. See? I was safe behind the glass, and a guard was with me. I'm fine. I promise."

His anger seemed to fizzle, and he gave a slow nod of acceptance. "You're right. I'm sorry. You're a grown woman, and I know I don't have any say in what you can and can't do, but I do worry about you, Jillian. Especially given your penchant for trouble. But I should have just told you that instead of flying off the handle like I did. Forgive me?"

His expression was so contrite that she complied instantly. "Of course."

"Can you tell me what you were looking for? I could have helped you get it."

Jillian shook her head. "You couldn't have gotten this for me."

"Try me."

"All right. I needed to see his face when I asked him if he did it."

"You're right—I couldn't have gotten that. Why did you want it?"

"Gooder stopped by yesterday morning. He seemed to be implying that I was a suspect, just like you told me."

"I didn't say you were a suspect. I said the police would want to ask you some questions about the photo."

"That's enough for me to care. They've suspected me in the past, remember?" She glanced at the bakery door, suspicious that Bertie and Lenora had abandoned their tasks and were stationed on the other side of the door, each one holding a drinking glass against it with an ear pressed to the other end. The main evidence against that theory was that Bertie hadn't yet burst from the building to scold Jillian for going to the jail the night before. Just to be safe from eavesdroppers, Jillian lowered her voice, but her words were full of conviction as she confided the idea that had plagued her the previous night. "Jeremiah Davis didn't do it."

Confusion clouded Hunter's face. "But I thought you believed he was guilty."

"He's a thief, yes. His past precedes him. And I would be lying if I said I wasn't afraid of him at any point last night, but something didn't feel right."

"I'm going to ignore the fact that you just said you were in fear of an accused murderer while visiting a jail because I'm trying to be cool about this." The comment had a touch of humor that outweighed the mild rebuke. "Why don't you share a few more details about your theory?"

"He's adamant that someone is setting him up. And he claimed someone planted the wallet."

"Sounds like a man who doesn't want to go to prison to me."

"No, this was different. He thought I killed Sterling, or at least that I had some involvement in it. He accused *me* of being a part of the plan. But that's not all that makes me think he's innocent."

"His innocence is not for you to prove or disprove, Jillian." Hunter sighed. "Sorry. Go ahead, spill. Why else do you think he's innocent?"

"It was something in his eyes. They were distrustful. At first, he was angry, but he couldn't hide the fact that he really believes he can't trust anyone."

"He's a con man. He hangs with other cons. They know the deal: trust no one, especially an uninvited stranger coming to visit you in jail."

Jillian stared down the alley, watching an empty candy bar wrapper skitter across the ground in the breeze. "Maybe, but I'm still going to try to find out who he really is." She turned back. "And don't try to stop me."

Hunter laughed. "I am well aware that trying to stop you would be a futile endeavor."

"Good."

"But you have to let me help. No more slinking off into the night to dangerous places without telling anyone. Especially Bertie."

"She doesn't need to kn—"

Hunter interrupted her with a wry grin. "She already knows. Who do you think told me?"

Jillian scowled. "How did she find out? Oh, never mind." Of course Bertie knew. Nothing got past her, especially not her granddaughter popping by the local jail. "And . . . did she *tattle* on me to my boyfriend?"

Hunter gave a full belly laugh at that. "I suppose she did."

"We will be having a talk about that," Jillian said grimly. "As for you, Mr. Greyson, if you're so inclined as to help me get to the bottom of all this, you can offer assistance in scoping out information about Sterling Macon."

"The newspaper article about his passing was pretty vague. Sounds like boarding schools and Ivy League college and stuffy country clubs. No family, just an unnamed guardian who facilitated everything until he came of age. Kind of sad, really."

"His path must have crossed Jeremiah's at some point. Besides, Jeremiah confirmed what I thought already. Sterling was scamming me with that whole nut-allergy bit. Why would an Ivy League graduate from the country club set need to pull something like that?"

"Boredom?"

"He was dating Flannery Garland. How boring could his life be? She doesn't seem the type to settle for monotony."

"But she will settle for money." Bertie's voice startled both Jillian and Hunter.

Jillian whirled around and put a hand on her hip. "Don't you have better things to do than listen to a private conversation?"

"Don't you have better things to do than hightail it down to the jail and get yourself mixed up with who knows what sorts of criminals?" Bertie scoffed. "For goodness' sake, Jillian, you could have been killed."

"Funny thing about prisons—they actually don't let the inmates have weapons." Jillian rolled her eyes.

"I think I'd better let the two of you sort this out," Hunter said. "Jillian, I'll see you later. Goodbye, Bertie."

"Chicken," Jillian muttered as she watched him walk away. She turned back toward Bertie, wondering whether it was more daunting to find a killer or to face her irate grandmother.

The rest of Tuesday and all of Wednesday went by in a blur of special orders and unusually busy traffic at the bakery. With school out, lots of kids were buzzing in and out for doughnuts and cookies. It had been a hot day that had sapped Jillian's energy, and she couldn't wait for a cool shower and a cold salad. However, as she trudged into Belle Haven after her closing shift on Wednesday, she realized that she hadn't yet had a chance to do much digging on Sterling Macon beyond what Hunter had told her the previous morning.

After refreshing herself with a shower and throwing together some vegetables and a vinaigrette, Jillian took her salad bowl into her small office and fired up the computer. She brought up her own social media page, and then searched for one belonging to Sterling Macon. His photo came up first in the results, and Jillian's stomach did a little flip at seeing the dead con man gazing out at her from his profile picture. She clicked onto the page, but either his account was set to "private" or he didn't post much. He'd joined the site less than a year before, and the only public post was disturbingly familiar.

It was the photo he'd taken of Jillian from outside the bakery. As a caption, he'd written: *Lier, Lier, Choclate Shop Bakery on fire. This lady sold me a cookie ful of nuts after I told her I was deadly allergc. Reaction culd have killed me. Boycot this bakery or risk death.*

Taken aback almost as much by the typos as she was by the vitriol behind the post, Jillian hurriedly scanned through the rest of the page but found no other information. Nothing indicated that Sterling had an Ivy League education, least of all his post about the bakery.

On a whim, Jillian searched Flannery Garland's name and came across what could only be described as the complete opposite type of profile. Flannery's public page was filled with links related to her work as a pageant queen, cute kitten videos, and photo after photo of the smiling beauty with other girls her age as well as her father, Earle Garland, and Lucinda Atwood.

Jillian didn't see any reference to Sterling Macon, but considering the private nature of his page, she wondered if he'd asked Flannery not to link to him. *I guess a con man wouldn't want his name tossed around by somebody with over 2,000 friends.*

Realizing she'd forgotten to check how many online connections Sterling himself had, Jillian hit her browser's back button to refresh his profile. She was met with an error message. *Page not found.*

That was strange. She tried searching for him again, but she only came up with Sterling Macons living in Nebraska, Idaho, and Australia—nowhere near Moss Hollow, Georgia.

Whether it was the shower, the salad, or something else entirely, Jillian's blood went cool at the thought that somebody out there had deleted Sterling's page. What other evidence of his existence might they try to get rid of next?

Thursday morning ticked by quickly into the lunch hour, although Jillian was so caught up in work that she barely checked the clock. Lenora had cracked a tooth and made an emergency trip to the dentist, and Jillian and Bertie had shifted into overdrive to pick up the slack.

Shortly after two o'clock, Maggie bustled into the kitchen to grab a special order. She stopped short when she passed Jillian. "Did you know that Hunter has been sitting out front for over an hour?"

Pausing in the act of portioning off dinner rolls, Jillian wiped her forehead with the back of a flour-covered hand. "He has?"

Maggie nodded. "I asked him if he wanted me to come get you, but he said he'd just wait."

Jillian glanced down at the mound of dough in front of her. "Well he'll have to wait a few more minutes, I guess. I'll be out shortly."

After Maggie retreated, Jillian finished forming her rolls and put them in the proofer. She hustled out to the front of the bakery. She couldn't help but smile when she saw Hunter reading a newspaper at a table in the corner, an empty dessert plate in front of him. He appeared to have made himself quite at home for the last hour.

"Don't you have work to do?" she teased.

He glanced up and returned her smile, then seemed to bite back a chuckle. "You're apparently working hard enough for the both of us. It's all over your face."

"What?" Jillian squinted at her reflection in the window and rolled her eyes when she saw the smear of flour across her forehead. She accepted the napkin Hunter offered and wiped her face clean. "Thanks for the heads-up. Now what can I do for you?"

"Actually, it's more what I can do for you. I have the afternoon free. I thought we could head out to Beech Brook."

"I'm afraid I'm a little busy for a recreational drive in the country. What's so special about a town two counties away?"

"You said you wanted to do a little research on our suspect. That's where he's from."

"Well, why didn't you say so?" Intrigued, Jillian pulled up a chair and sat down. "What did you find out?"

"Not much yet. I thought we could head to the town hall and see if we can have a look at their records. They close at five. We could be there with time to spare if we leave now."

The bells over the door chimed. Reminded of the pile of work waiting for her in back, Jillian sighed. Duty called. "I wish I could take off, but Lenora's out today and I can't leave Bertie here alone."

Hunter gazed past Jillian to someone behind her. "Don't be so sure."

Jillian twisted around to see Savannah standing there, sweet smile in place.

"I'm reporting to work, boss." Savannah gave a mock salute. "Where do you need me?"

Jillian swung back around to catch Hunter's satisfied grin. "You did this?" At his shrug, she asked, "But why? You were so set against me doing some research before. What's changed?"

"If you can't beat 'em, join 'em." His smile faltered. "I still think it's dangerous. You could get hurt, but there's strength in numbers. If I'm there, I'll be less worried about you."

"I would never put myself in harm's way," Jillian said. Behind her, Savannah snorted, and Jillian sent her a glare. "Okay, I would never *intentionally* put myself in harm's way. I just want to find out how these men know each other."

"A man is dead, don't forget." Hunter gave his attention to Savannah. "Thank you for coming."

"Anytime. I cleared my schedule for the rest of the day, so don't worry about hurrying back."

Jillian stood to give her friend a hug of gratitude. "Thank you, Savannah."

Savannah returned the embrace warmly. "That's what friends are for. Now get out of here."

An hour later, Hunter pulled his dark silver Lexus off of the interstate and into a town that had seen better days. Jillian's heart broke a little as they drove down Beech Brook's main drag. There were more storefronts boarded up than open. A laundromat with two ladies sitting by its dingy glass window seemed to be the most hopping place. One of the patrons had a magazine brought up close to her face, but as Hunter's car drove by, she flipped the cover down just enough to see who was at the wheel, her eyes in a suspicious squint.

"We're not in Moss Hollow anymore," Jillian mumbled, slinking down a bit in the passenger's seat. "What do you suppose happened here?"

"My guess is a change in the employment rate," Hunter said. "When people have money coming in, they feel safe enough to spend it. When they spend it, stores stay in business."

A young boy in a green baseball cap sat on the curb ahead, a skateboard resting nearby. He was drawing a stick through the dirt collected on the side of the road. He lifted a smudged face to them as they passed slowly. His head tilted as he stood and his reddish-brown hair stuck out beneath the cap. A pair of intense brown eyes peered at Jillian from beneath the brim.

"Stop the car," Jillian said. "Let's talk to that kid."

Hunter huffed. "I don't think that's a good idea."

"Oh, stop. He's just a boy. He can't be more than twelve years old."

"All right." Hunter slowed to a stop and put the car in park.

Jillian rolled her window down. "Excuse me, may I ask you a question?"

The boy shrugged, then warily looked across the street at the ladies in the laundromat window, both of whom were openly watching the scene playing out on the street. He kicked at the dirt, then said quietly, "What do you want?"

"Do you know a man named Jeremiah Davis?"

The boy's brow furrowed, and Jillian was about to take that as a no when he asked, "Oh, you mean J.D.?"

Jillian hesitated, unsure if that was who she meant at all. "Um, he plays piano. Does J.D. play piano?"

The boy glanced behind him down the street for only a moment, but it was long enough for Jillian to see what captured his attention.

She read the hanging neon sign aloud. "'Ken's Piano Bar.'

Thanks, buddy. We'll head there next." Before Jillian rolled up her window, she paused. "Are you hungry?"

The boy shrugged. "Maybe."

She opened her purse and withdrew a paper sack of chocolate chip cookies she had packed before she left the bakery. Passing them through the window to his eager hands, Jillian watched him devour one whole. She wanted to ask him when he had last eaten anything. Instead, she asked him his name.

"Paulie," he said, his mouth full.

"It was nice to meet you, Paulie. I'm Jillian, and this is Hunter."

"Are you cops?"

Jillian laughed, imagining Gooder's horror if he found out someone had asked her that. "No, not at all. I'm a baker. I made those cookies this morning in my bakery."

"They're good. Where's your bakery?"

"About an hour from here, in Moss Hollow. Ever heard of it?"

Paulie shook his head and took a smaller bite this time.

"It's called The Chocolate Shoppe Bakery."

A smile twitched on the boy's lips. "I like the sound of that."

Jillian beamed at Paulie. "Most people do. If you're ever in Moss Hollow, you're welcome to stop by for more cookies."

"You bet I will." His excited eyes showed no more wariness. "Bye, Jillian. Bye, Hunter."

With that, Paulie kicked up his skateboard in a smooth move. In another instant, he was on the board and coasting down the street. He took a fast corner and disappeared down an alleyway.

"I hope he has a safe place to go," Jillian said.

Hunter put his warm hand on hers. "I love the way you care for people. You have a beautiful heart, Jillian."

Jillian's face flushed at the compliment. "You're not so bad yourself."

Hunter responded with a smile, then drew his hand away

and put the car in gear. He pulled into a parking space and cut the engine.

The warm sensation left by Hunter's hand slipped away quickly as Jillian mentally prepared herself for what was next. Asking a kid on the street about Jeremiah was one thing. Sauntering into a seedy piano bar to dig up dirt on one of its employees was something else entirely.

"Are you ready?" Hunter asked.

"As I'll ever be." She glanced at the purse on her lap. "Maybe I'd better leave this here." After tucking the handbag under her seat, Jillian climbed out and joined Hunter on the sidewalk. Together, they approached the piano bar, which was wedged between a shuttered nail salon on one side and a long-gone record shop on the other. Hunter pulled on the door, and it opened with a disgruntled creak. They entered together.

Jillian blinked to adjust her eyes to the dark interior of the piano bar, not to mention the haze of smoke that irritated her eyes. She struggled to keep her eyelids open past half-mast, wishing she could hold her nose against the musty odor that assaulted her.

The bar, backed by rows of bottles lined up in front of a cloudy mirror, stood off to the right of the long, narrow room. A baby grand piano sat at the back of the bar, indicating that, despite all appearances, the music hadn't died completely in this desolate town.

But how long could it last without Jeremiah Davis around to play?

Hunter led the way to the bar, where a woman with straight black hair chewed on the eraser end of a pencil. Her face was shielded by a few loose locks as she hovered over some papers on the counter.

"Excuse us," Hunter said. "Do you have a moment?"

The woman shifted her face to take them in, but remained

bent over whatever she was studying. "What'll you have?" she asked, her voice grinding like a machine in need of grease.

Hunter shook his head, but Jillian cut him off. "Two seltzers, please."

The woman eyed her almost suspiciously, then said, "Coming up." She dropped her pencil and went to the fountain to slosh up two foggy glasses.

Jillian could only hope they'd seen a dishwasher sometime in the last few weeks, but took the glass with a smile.

"Thank you." She claimed one of the vacant bar stools and nodded to Hunter to follow her lead. After he placed a five-dollar bill on the counter, he sat beside her and took his first sip. Jillian saw the bartender had returned to her work. "Excuse me," Jillian called out.

"We don't serve food until five," the barkeep answered before Jillian could ask another question.

"Actually, I was wondering if Jeremiah Davis played here."

"When he decides to grace us with his presence," she replied caustically. "J.D.'s been off playing for high-society folks. Can't be bothered to remember us little people. But mark my words—he'll come crawling back when he learns who his real friends are, instead of those fakes who are just using him. We were all he had for a good long while. Rich people don't stick to their friends the way we do."

So, does that mean the woman has heard about Jeremiah's arrest, or hasn't? Jillian glanced at the piano sitting at the ready and pictured Jeremiah's long fingers dancing across the keys.

"Doesn't matter," the bartender said, continuing her tirade. "We have other players who understand the importance of remembering their roots. Isn't that right, Ruben?"

Jillian squinted and gazed around the room. She hadn't thought there was anyone else in the place.

"It serves them well to." A jagged tenor voice lifted from a booth at the back. A swirl of fresh smoke drifted to the ceiling, and the tip of a cigarette lit up as the man inhaled deeply from it. It was enough illumination to catch a glimpse of his dark face in the shadows, and Jillian saw that he wore sunglasses. *To protect from what light?* she wondered, glancing around the gloomy bar.

The entrance door opened, pouring daylight inside for the few brief seconds it took the two patrons to come inside. The woman shrieked with laughter at something the guy had said. They held hands and scanned the dimly lit room.

"Let's sit near the piano," the woman said. The two paraded over and made themselves comfortable, then put their heads together in their own private conversation.

Hunter leaned over the bar and asked the bartender, "Do you know a man named Sterling Macon?"

The barkeep's instant perplexed look said she wasn't lying when she replied, "Never heard of him."

Hunter took out a picture of Sterling—*I'm glad one of us came prepared*, Jillian thought—and passed it over to the dark-haired woman. Her eyes shifted in the direction of Ruben's table. She slid the photo back toward them. "Nope, never saw that man in my life. Excuse me, I have to get back to work." She grabbed her pencil and a pad from her apron and hustled from behind the bar. She approached the couple by the piano with what appeared to be a newfound enthusiasm for her job.

Jillian and Hunter passed glances of speculation. Had the bartender recognized the photo of Sterling? Perhaps she knew him, but by a different name.

Jillian grabbed the picture and swiveled around to face the man in the shadows. "How about you? Would you be willing to see if the man in this picture is familiar to you?"

The cigarette burned bright again. Ruben exhaled swirls of smoke. "I think I will have to pass."

The entrance swung wide again with another man at the door. Instead of taking a seat at a table, however, he went straight to the piano and took the seat at the keys. Jeremiah's replacement had arrived.

"Sorry I'm late, friends." The pianist's fingers quickly trilled out a scale. "You'd think I'd have all the time in the world being out of work and all, but I've been hitting the pavement for a new job, and that pavement has been leading me far and wide, man." His fingers dallied up and down the keyboard as he continued to warm up. "Days like this, I miss working at Fugue Labs. But don't we all?"

The cigarette lit up again from the back booth, the only response in the hazy bar.

The pianist started playing odds and ends of jazz songs. "Welcome to Ken's Piano Bar. Thank you for coming out to hear some tunes. I take requests and tips, and I'm here to listen to your woes. Gather around, folks. My name is Travis, and there's nowhere I'd rather be. Except at a real job of course." He tipped the sparse audience a wink, and there were a couple of low chuckles.

Hunter leaned close. "Are you ready to move on? We don't have a lot of time before the town hall closes."

Jillian nodded. She was getting the sense that they weren't going to learn much from the people at Ken's. Ruben barely talked, the bartender was now conspicuously avoiding them, and Travis had a show to do. As she followed Hunter to the door, the piano man embarked on a familiar bluesy number that had goosebumps jumping up on Jillian's skin.

She paused at the door. Hunter held it wide for her, but she hesitated. There was something about the song.

"You ready?" Hunter asked.

"I guess so, but that song . . ."

"What about it?"

Jillian shook her head and walked through the doorway and onto the sidewalk. Hunter turned toward his car, but she stayed put, silently trying to puzzle out what was so disconcerting about that tune. She inhaled as a memory hit her. "Jeremiah played that song at the fund-raiser. Do you remember it?"

Hunter shrugged. "Maybe. It's Ray Charles, right?"

"Yes, but that's not what matters. Jeremiah also started his show with it."

"Well, maybe it's the boss's favorite, and he expects his piano players to know it."

"I wonder if he knows about Jeremiah. I want to ask him."

"Jillian, Ken's Piano Bar does not strike me as the place to get information. And I really don't think it's safe."

Jillian swung around. "I'll be right back. I just need to ask him something real quick."

"Wait, I'll come with—"

"No, you stay here. I'll be fine." She pulled the door open and disappeared back inside the dark cavern.

Travis banged out rhythm and the blues coupled with a gospel flair on the ivory keys. As Jillian approached the piano, the player watched her every move. She took a vacant chair to the side and didn't interrupt his song. At a lull, she decided to chance an innocent question.

"Do you like peach pie?" she asked.

A slight smile curved Travis's mouth, but his playing didn't miss a beat. He transitioned skillfully from a lively tune into a slow rendition of "Georgia on My Mind."

If Jillian planned to dig deeper, the time was now. "Do you know the other piano guy who plays here? Jeremiah Davis?"

The music jarred to a stop, and the piano player cast a lethal glare on her. She shrank back in her chair as far as she could, hoping her face didn't give away her misgivings for returning to the dark bar teeming with secrets.

Travis's eyes flickered away from her as he cast a quick glance around the silent bar. Jillian did the same. The laughing couple ducked their heads and found more interest in their drinks than they had before. Swirling smoke stopped drifting to the ceiling where Ruben sat in his booth. Jillian squirmed in her seat as she caught a scathing look from the bartender, the glass in her hand gripped in white knuckles.

Jillian faced the man at the keys again. "I just want to know if you've heard what happened to Jeremiah Davis. I'm trying to help him."

A bead of sweat slipped down from Travis's right temple, but he didn't respond. Jillian took a deep breath, wondering if her last shot at finding out anything was Ruben. Before she could make a move, the music began again.

Without taking his eyes off her, the piano man's fingers slowly picked up and moved into another song, no longer the sweet notes of "Georgia on My Mind" but the heavy percussive sounds of Ray Charles's song "Busted."

Busted?

As in, Travis knew Jeremiah had been arrested? Or was this message indicating that Jillian herself was the one in trouble?

Jillian sat frozen in place, not sure whether to ask Travis another question, make for the rather inviting exit door, or attempt to talk to the mysterious smoking man in the corner.

Before she could come to a decision, Hunter reentered the bar. Seeing him gave her the resolve she needed to continue her search for information.

She reached into her pocket and pulled out the photo of Sterling Macon. "Do you know this man?" She held the photo up toward Travis, but if he looked at it, she couldn't tell. His only response was to speed up his playing and seamlessly transition into another song. This one spread his message loud and clear. She sang the lyrics in her head.

Hit the road, Jack, and don't you come back no more.

Hunter took the seat beside her and leaned close to speak into her ear. "You're not going to get anything out of this guy. Let's try the town hall. They might be more cooperative."

Jillian had little hope of finding out anything in this town full of sullen, silent strangers. And she was out of bribes—she'd given all her cookies to Paulie.

"I'm not a cop, and neither is he," she told the piano player, nodding at Hunter. "We're here because I think an innocent man is behind bars. Jeremiah Davis is in jail. I don't know if he's a friend of yours, but either way, he's going to need people to speak for him. I was hoping that you would be one of them."

Travis kept his mouth shut and cast his eyes down to face the piano keys. Jillian finally gave up. She and Hunter rose from their chairs and made their way to the door. Just as Hunter was pulling on the knob, the song changed to another of Ray Charles's greatest hits, "I Wonder Who's Kissing Her Now."

They stepped outside into the warm sunshine, so blinding that Jillian squinted in pain. Behind the closed door, she could hear the music play on, and she heard Ray Charles's voice in her head, singing about a girl moving on into another's arms.

Another message, perhaps?

If so, then who was the girl Travis was playing about? Who was kissing another man? Who was the first man who got kicked to the curb?

Jillian looked down at the photo in her hands. Sterling scowled up at her.

No, not kicked to the curb. Knifed in the tulips. In an instant,

Jillian realized just who the girl in the song was supposed to be—Flannery Garland.

"Are you coming?" Hunter called from down the block next to his car. "The town hall will close soon."

Jillian nodded and jogged toward him. "I have an idea of what we should check into when we get back to Moss Hollow."

"What's that?" He opened the car door for her.

She stepped a foot into the Lexus, then turned to Hunter, batting her eyelashes. In her best Scarlett O'Hara drawl, she said, "Why, Mr. Greyson, we need to find out who Flannery Garland is kissing now."

"This is where Jeremiah Davis lives?" Jillian assessed the rows of trailers strewn before her, many in desperate need of repair. As Hunter rolled slowly through the unpaved street of the Glory Days Trailer Park, his tires kicked up loose sand and rock in slow crunches.

"According to the town hall's records, this place is his last known address." Hunter stopped the car and put it in park. A rundown trailer worse than any other in the park stood—just barely—outside Jillian's window. "I'd say its glory days are memories now."

Jillian agreed. "The place looks abandoned. I guess the pay for playing piano at Ken's isn't up to par."

"If what the bartender said about Jeremiah moving on from his roots was true, I can't say I blame him. Especially after what the lady at the town hall said."

"Losing a parent as a teenager would be hard for anyone, but to be left to take care of your sick mother and younger sisters with no money?" Jillian shook her head. "I can't imagine."

"Sounds like he's had it rough for a long time."

Jillian nodded at Hunter's remark and climbed out of the car. She grabbed her cell phone from her purse and took a few photos of the front of the trailer. The grass tickled her calves as she stepped through the overgrowth to peer into a cloudy window.

Surprisingly neat, she thought. Its furniture was sparse, but what was inside had been taken care of. Especially the upright piano. "It actually has a homey feel to it in there, as if he made the best of his circumstances."

Hunter stepped up beside her to take a peek. "A neat home doesn't mean he's not a killer."

"Doesn't mean he is one either." Jillian moved along the side of the trailer. As she did, a quick movement in the neighboring trailer's window caught her attention. A cotton curtain blocked her view, but she knew without a doubt that someone had been watching. "Let's go knock on the neighbor's door."

"For what?"

"Character reference." Jillian left the long grass for the better-kept yard next door. She rapped on the metal screen door a few times, seeming to rattle the whole structure. "Hello?" Silence met her. "I just wanted to ask you a few things about your neighbor, Jeremiah. Or J.D., however you knew him. Would you mind?"

Still no response came.

"Please." Jillian tried once more, pleading in her voice. "It's very important."

"Is he dead?" An old woman's voice crackled out through the screened windows, but the door remained closed.

"No, he's not." Jillian wondered why that was the woman's first question. "Why would you say that?"

"It's only a matter of time. He's made the wrong enemies."

Hunter raised his eyebrows at Jillian and appeared ready to say something, but she shot him a silencing glare.

"Could you name some of those enemies?" Jillian asked. "Jeremiah's not dead, but he is in trouble. Your help could make the difference for him."

"The list is too long. That boy strayed from the straight and narrow. Got a little taste of success too many times. I always worried it spoiled him for anything legit. Why would he go straight? The money was too good not to keep trying. I figured eventually he would either strike it rich or get struck dead from going after the wrong person."

Jillian reached into her pocket for Sterling Macon's photo. "Like this person?" She held up the photo to the window beside the door.

"Definitely like that person. The two of them hated each other."

Jillian's suspicion that the two men worked together on scams may have been unfounded if they hated each other. "Do you know where Sterling was from?"

"Who?"

"The man in the picture. Sterling Macon. Do you know where he was from?"

Something crashed inside the trailer. "What do you mean where he *was* from? Is Bo dead? Is that what you're telling me?"

Jillian lost the conversation. "I'm sorry, did you say Bo? Who's Bo?"

"Get lost before I call the cops! I've got a gun!"

Hunter reached for Jillian's arm, but she was already down the steps and making her way back to the car. She threw herself into her seat as Hunter did the same and started his car in a hurry. They exited the trailer park with a spray of dust and sand shooting out from their tires, and neither spoke until the wheels hit pavement and signs for the highway beckoned ahead.

"The woman was scared. That's all. She wouldn't have shot us." The tremor in Jillian's voice belied her words.

"Not a chance I was willing to take." Hunter hit a button on his steering wheel. "Call office," he instructed the hands-free phone system.

After a few rings, a woman answered loudly. "Greyson & Sons."

Jillian glanced Hunter's way in confusion. That was not the voice of his usual assistant, Oliver Kent.

Hunter whispered, "Oliver's out of town. This is his fill-in, Valerie Winston." He raised his voice to respond to the substitute assistant. "Valerie, it's Hunter."

"Hi, boss. Phone calls at the end of my workday only mean one thing: It's *not* the end of my workday after all. Am I right?"

"Unfortunately. I'm out of town, and I need you to do something for me."

"That's okay. I only had a once-in-a-lifetime date I've been looking forward to for a week, but what do you need?"

"You won't miss your date, I promise. All I need you to do is take Sterling Macon's fingerprints."

"That's not protocol."

"It is if that corpse in the morgue isn't really named Sterling Macon."

Silence filled the car.

"Did you hear me, Val?"

Suddenly Val squealed. "You've got to be kidding me! I forgive you about messing with my date. I'll get right on it. Oliver is gonna be sore he missed this."

"Tell the sheriff to run them right away."

"Not my first rodeo, boss." The line went dead.

Hunter glanced at Jillian. "Don't let the sass fool you. She really is smart and efficient. She'll get it done in record time."

Jillian had no doubt, but still bit back a smile. "She sounds interesting."

"She's got some spunk, for sure."

"When do you think she'll get the prints back?" Jillian asked.

Hunter took the entrance ramp for the highway. "Well, typically it could take twenty minutes. Or it could be twenty days."

Twenty days? Jillian took a deep breath and accepted that she might have to continue her search without the information. "Maybe Bo is just a nickname for Sterling," she said aloud.

"The woman didn't recognize the name you gave her. I don't think she knew him as Sterling Macon."

Jillian sighed and watched the trees speed by her window.

"Whoever he was, that lady was scared of him. And scared of us for asking questions about him."

"That's what's making me nervous. I wish you'd give up this case, Jillian. Let the police handle it. It goes much deeper and is more dangerous than I thought. We're not just dealing with a couple of competing con artists here."

Jillian felt a stinging pain from her lower lip and realized she was biting it. She made herself stop and asked, "Do you think Flannery knew her fiancé wasn't who he said he was?"

"Maybe she found out and couldn't let it ruin her—" Hunter paused, glancing in the rearview mirror. He squinted at what he saw. "Hang on."

"Why?" Jillian craned her neck to peer behind them.

"Because there's a limo that's been behind me since we got on the interstate. I'm going to try to lose it." Hunter hit the gas pedal, sending Jillian's head back on her headrest.

Who's being reckless now? Jillian checked her side mirror and saw the edge of a sleek black car edging dangerously close to the Lexus's rear bumper. The mirror warned of objects appearing closer than reality, but a quick glance out the back window told her that the limo really was right on their tail.

"They're keeping up with us," she informed Hunter as she squinted to make out the driver's face. The sun glinted off the windshield, protecting the driver's identity.

Hunter floored the gas pedal and maneuvered his car into the right lane between two semitrailers. Watching her mirror, Jillian waited for the black car to come up on their left, but the car disappeared behind the rear truck and out of view.

They drove in heavy silence, sandwiched between the two large trucks, until Hunter slowed his car and took an exit without warning. Jillian watched out the rear window to see the black car drive on, continuing down the highway without them.

Maybe the limousine had been following them, maybe not, but Jillian felt better not having it behind them regardless.

Hunter's mobile phone rang through the tense atmosphere inside the Lexus. He hit the answer button on the steering wheel. "What did you find out, Val?"

"Well, I have to draw paperwork for a new dead guy. Our victim's name is not Sterling Macon."

"Would it happen to be Bo?"

"What do you need me for, if you already know?"

"I'm sorry," Hunter said with humor in his voice. "Go ahead."

"His name is Bo Randall Tyler, and he has a rap sheet a mile long. Dangerous stuff. I know he's dead, but I'm a little uncomfortable being in the building with him."

Jillian quickly typed the name Bo Tyler into the search engine on her smartphone. Where the name Sterling Macon had brought up only a barren social media profile, this search went on for pages. But Jillian only needed one for confirmation. Attached to an article about an armed robbery a few counties over was a mug shot of Bo Tyler. From it, Sterling Macon stared at her with the same lethal look he had given her the day he came to the bakery.

After dinner at Crazy Fish Bar & Grille with Hunter, Jillian arrived at Belle Haven to find Cornelia and Possum lounging in the library. Somehow, Cornelia had managed to fit both the fluffy cat and a large hardcover novel in her lap.

Cornelia glanced up and smiled. "Did you have a nice afternoon with your beau?"

Jillian plopped down next to her great-aunt and used her phone to pull up the site with Bo Tyler's mug shot. "You might find this more intriguing than your novel." Jillian turned the screen so Cornelia could see what they had discovered during the excursion. "I wouldn't say it was a nice afternoon, but it was certainly informative."

Cornelia urged Possum off her lap, ignoring the cat's disgruntled glare, and leaned over to examine the photo more closely. "Is that . . .?"

"Our dead guy? It sure is. Apparently his real name is Bo Tyler, and he was a full-time crook."

Cornelia jumped up and hustled over to the door. "Bertie!" she hollered. "Get in here right now."

Bertie stepped into the room holding a glass of sweet tea. "Sister, there really is no need to embarrass yourself with all that squalling."

"Wait until you see what Jillian found out today. You'll be yelling too."

Bertie stepped further into the room. "What did you find?"

Jillian stood and held her phone screen toward Bertie. "Sterling Macon is not Sterling Macon. He's Bo Tyler, and I think he was in the middle of conning the wrong person, and she killed him."

"*She?*" The twin sisters were mirror images of shock as they gaped at each other and then at Jillian.

"You think a woman killed him?" Cornelia asked. "Who?"

"My money right now is on Flannery," Jillian said. "Imagine her surprise if she learned her fiancé wasn't the man he pretended to be."

"You really think a beauty queen sank a knife into her man's back?" Cornelia asked.

"Well, she could have paid someone to do it." Jillian wasn't ready to relinquish her idea. "She comes from money, doesn't she?"

Bertie shook her head. "Plenty of people who were at that fund-raiser have the money. I think you need to dig deeper. Who else at that party might have known Sterling Macon wasn't who he said he was?"

A crash banged through the room, and the three women swiveled their heads to find the source of the noise. Next to the window, Possum sat nonchalantly beside a mess of dirt and terra-cotta chunks. He had knocked over a planter, scattering potting soil all over the floor.

Cornelia went for the cat. "Oh, Raymond, what are you up to?"

Bertie harrumphed. "*Possum* is up to typical cat behavior, like always."

"Oh, piffle. Raymond's trying to tell us something. I just know it."

"Yeah, like, 'It's time for my bacon,'" Jillian said, her heart still thumping after the startling incident.

"Fiddlesticks. What bacon?" Cornelia bent down to lift the cat's chin and stare into his blue eyes. "I know what will help." She scooped the puffball into her arms and headed out of the library.

"She thinks we don't notice all the bacon he gets," Bertie said. "I do the grocery shopping. I know how much bacon we have and eat, and I know a lot goes missing. That cat is going to get fat."

Jillian smirked and went to retrieve a broom and dustpan to clean up the mess. The storage closet came up empty though. She peeked her head back in the library. "Any idea where the broom is?"

Bertie put a hand to her cheek. "I'm sorry, dear. I was using it to sweep the front porch. I must have left it out there."

"No problem. I'll be right back."

Jillian opened the manor's front door and quickly spotted the broom leaning against a column by the steps. Belle Haven's grand two-story porch spanned the whole front of the mansion and wrapped around both ends to enclose the front rooms. A destination on warm summer nights and for beautiful sunsets, the front porch filled the role of Southern hospitality. Many house visits with friends took place on the ornate furniture pieces with sweet tea and cakes.

With the sun already set, Jillian bypassed the plush sofa and headed back to the front door, broom in hand.

As she reached for the handle, her attention fell to a white slip of paper stuck to the wooden door. The paper was taped at an angle, dead center, as though someone had been in a rush when they had slapped it there.

Jillian pivoted to scan the vast acreage of darkness in front of Belle Haven. She didn't expect to see anything past the front steps, but the hair prickling at the base of her neck made her check anyway. Especially because the paper wasn't blank. Scrawled haphazardly across the paper was one solitary sentence. A warning for no one but her.

Stick to baking or else.

Jillian ripped it off the door and crumpled it in her hand. She glanced behind her again, but stepped inside as she did. As she closed and locked the door and leaned against it, she looked down at the wad of paper in her hand. A few feet away, Possum sat on his haunches. He let out a loud meow and got up to weave between her legs.

"I guess you really were trying to tell us something, weren't you, Possum? Someone had been here, and you knew it." Jillian knelt down to scratch the cat beneath his chin. Fear stalled her drive to seek justice, and right now she was grateful not to be alone through it. Her fingers dug deep into Possum's warm fur, and she let his purrs soothe her. "I wish Cornelia was right, and you really could tell me what to do. Do I stop trying to find a killer and accept that the bad guy is already behind bars? But if the real murderer has already been caught, why am I getting this note?"

At Possum's answering meow, Jillian stood and nodded, her resolve strengthened. "That's what I think too."

By noon on Friday, Jillian's nerves had relaxed and she was ready to dive back into her investigation during a slow period at the bakery. She called Hunter on his cell phone, but it went to voice mail. Part of her was glad. She didn't think he'd be too keen on her next move.

Jillian walked through the door of the county jail, hoping she looked more confident than she felt. Inside, the same female guard from the last visit sat at the desk.

"Jeremiah Davis?" she asked, grabbing a clipboard and holding it out for Jillian to sign.

Jillian took it and scrawled her name and signature in the allotted spaces. "Sorry, I forgot to ask him something."

The guard raised her eyebrows in question. "Are you sure it's wise? The last time didn't end too well."

"I guess I'll find out soon enough."

Jillian rubbed sweating palms down her linen slacks and paced through the waiting room until the guard returned, holding the door for her to enter.

The guard gave her a nod. "It took some doing, but he'll see you again."

The walk through the metal door showed Jeremiah already in his chair, phone receiver in hand. At the glass window, she expected another blowup or hateful response, but Jeremiah only watched her pensively.

She picked the visitor phone up off the cradle and took her seat. "Hello again," she said.

"Nice to see you still alive," came his reply.

She stared at him in surprise. "Should I not be?"

"Something tells me you're still snooping. You didn't heed my warning."

"You mean your threat."

"Whatever it takes to get you back to baking."

"Or else?" she responded, using the same words that had been on the note. Except it couldn't have been Jeremiah who had left it for her. He was behind bars.

Jeremiah nodded. "Glad to see you know the consequences. But I guess you don't care about those, or you wouldn't be here."

"Does the name Bo Tyler mean anything to you?"

Jeremiah said nothing, but his jaw tightened.

"I'll take it you already knew his real name," Jillian said. "Why didn't you say so to the police?"

Jeremiah looked behind her to the guard at the door. He leaned close and spoke in a whisper. "Please stop. Go home. Go back to your life. Go bake something. Just stop this search. These are not people who play fair. Or safe. Trust me, I should know. They're thieves and liars, and always will be."

"You're a thief."

"Yes."

"You're a liar."

"Most definitely."

"But you're not a killer."

Jeremiah stilled. He leaned back in his chair with an exasperated sigh. "Why are you doing this?"

"Because I don't think you killed your friend. And, if I'm being completely honest, you don't strike me as a murderer."

"That's mighty charitable of you, but you need to get one thing straight: Bo Tyler was not my friend. In this business, you don't make friends. Especially when you set out to ruin the other's game."

"Bo tried to ruin your scam?"

"No. I ruined one of his."

"Is it possible he's the one who set you up?"

"For stealing that wallet, maybe. But he was more likely to stick that knife in my back than to make it look like I did it to him. He's not even here to enjoy seeing me in this rotten place. I keep thinking it was made up. That he's not really dead. He's off somewhere laughing his fool head off."

"Oh, he's dead all right. His body is at the coroner's. His fingerprints proved his identity."

Jeremiah released a deep breath of frustration. He rubbed his forehead vigorously. He let out a growl through the phone, and Jillian heard his fight against defeat come through. She wanted to tell him that it wasn't over yet, but from where he sat, she doubted he would agree. If the police gathered enough evidence to charge and convict him, Jeremiah's record would keep him behind bars for a long time, even life.

But Bo's sentence had been death.

As corrupt as the man was, Jillian doubted he'd give up his life for anything, even taking down a sworn enemy.

"What was the scam you interfered with?" Jillian asked. "The one that set Bo Tyler off to come after you at the fund-raiser?"

"He goes after older folks. Widowed women, usually."

Jillian thought of Jeremiah's neighbor in the trailer park. She had feared Bo Tyler, enough to send her and Hunter away at the mention of him. Now Jillian understood why. The neighbor probably had firsthand experience with the con man because she or someone she knew had been on the receiving end of one of his scams. "I went to see your neighbor. She freaked when I said his name and told me she was armed."

Jeremiah arched his eyebrows. "You talked to Velma? You are one crazy broad. Are you *trying* to get yourself killed?"

"Not everyone recoils at my presence, you know. Like that young boy who skateboards along Main Street. What was his name? Oh yes, Paulie."

"You talked to Paulie?" Jeremiah's voice rose.

"He liked my cookies enough to swap some information."

Jeremiah shook his head. "That's bribery. You took advantage of a young boy who lost his father to cancer. Are you sure you're not the con man?"

Jillian frowned upon learning more about the boy's home life. "I wish I'd known. He was the only one who actually gave me information. He told me about the piano bar, but even the piano player wouldn't actually talk to me. He only played his piano in answer to my questions."

"Played?" Jeremiah clearly wasn't following.

"I think he was trying to give me clues through the songs he was playing. It sounds crazy, but it doesn't matter right now. Just tell me about the scam Bo tried to pull off. And how you kept him from succeeding."

Jeremiah frowned. "It was big. Bigger than he usually goes after. Corporate embezzling stuff."

"Embezzling?" Jillian felt nauseated. The very word dredged up memories of her ex-fiancé's crime and its aftermath.

"Yeah, I think he hooked up with someone for this one, someone with connections to the money. And a vendetta of their own. Lucinda never saw it coming."

"Lucinda Atwood?"

"That's right."

"How did you tell Lucinda that Bo was stealing from her?"

"I approached her at an event I was playing. I told her someone close to her was taking her for a ride and to look into the bosses at the place her husband owned. He died a few years back, and Beech Brook hasn't been the same since. The rest of the people in charge have been taking advantage of the workers. The ones they kept on payroll, anyway."

"People lost their jobs?"

Jeremiah nodded.

"I could see for myself that your town has seen better days." But Beech Brook's economic fallout wasn't why Jillian was here. She leaned in and lowered her voice. "I want to help you clear your name."

Jeremiah leaned in as well. "You can't help me at all. Go home and forget you ever met me."

"How did you get the gig at the fund-raiser?"

He straightened then shrugged. "Lucinda. She was grateful to me for alerting her in time before she lost everything. She made some changes and saved the business because of me."

"So she gave you a legitimate job."

"I suppose, but I've had others. Don't think I just go around committing crimes to live on."

"You mean working at Ken's? They can't pay much, if anything at all."

Jeremiah sent her a heated stare, but then gave a resigned nod. "Things will get better. Someone called the bar one night and said they'd like to hire me to play a few gigs. Ruben agreed to be my manager."

"So things are looking up," she said encouragingly.

"It just might be my golden ticket. If I ever get out of here."

Jillian frowned, remembering what his neighbor had said about him. He was always after the next big moneymaker, the next big scam that would be the one to either strike it rich or strike him dead.

"I hope you won't ruin it by stealing from the guests."

Jeremiah shrugged. "I hadn't thought of that."

"You're better than that, Jeremiah."

Anger distorted his facial features instantly. "You don't know anything about me."

"I know you helped a widow who was being scammed."

He avoided her gaze and gave no reply, not even a flicker of eyelashes. But she was sure this stone-cold demeanor was an act, and she pressed on.

"I know your father died when you were a teenager, and you were left to care for your mom and two siblings."

He raised his eyebrows in shock that she knew such a personal detail, then shifted and resumed his indifferent attitude. "So?"

"So was your mom scammed too?" It had been a guess, but his silence told her she'd been right. "It's the line you won't cross now. And you couldn't let Bo Tyler cross it either. That's why you alerted Lucinda, and why she hired you in gratitude."

"Gratitude? I'm in jail. And someone set me up to be here. How do I know this isn't what that old biddy actually considers her 'thank-you'?"

Jillian arched her eyebrows at Jeremiah. She hadn't thought of that, but honestly, she needed to consider everyone from that party as potential suspects. "You think she used you to take the fall for Tyler's murder? I suppose your reputation as a con man precedes you. If she wanted Tyler dead, what would it matter if another thief went down with him? She might even consider it doing her duty to rid society of lowlifes."

Jeremiah scoffed. "Why don't you tell me how you really feel about me?"

"Oh, sorry." Jillian waved her hand. "I didn't mean—"

He smirked. "It's fine. I'm a lowlife and I know it. There's nothing I can do about it."

Jillian frowned and wished she could change the way Jeremiah viewed himself. "Your home tells me otherwise," she said as she stood to take her leave. "You appreciate what you have and take care of it."

"I don't have much."

"It's not about quantity. It's about appreciation. Your appreciation is what sets you apart."

"From other lowlifes." His smile relaxed her enough to offer a smile in return.

"Maybe. But if Lucinda really did arrange for you to go down for murdering her con man just because of your reputation, then all the money in the world won't keep her from being the real lowlife."

Balancing a large bakery box in one hand and opening the door of the Clip & Curl Salon with the other, Jillian inhaled the pungent mix of flowery fragrances mixed with sharp chemicals from hair relaxers and dyes. The bell jingled overhead, and she headed to a row of comfortable chairs off to the side. Three salon chairs were filled with customers chatting away with their hairstylists. The stylist closest to the door glanced up at the sound of the bell. It was Jasmine Jackson, Lenora's cousin and the owner of the salon.

"Hi Jillian," she said. "Do you have an appointment today?"

Jillian raised the bakery box for Jasmine to see. "No, Lenora asked me to bring by the cake for your sister's birthday. She worked today but her mouth is still bugging her after her trip to the dentist. She wanted to nap after her shift so she's fresh for the party, but I'm here with the cake now in case she doesn't make it out of bed." Jillian set the box on the counter. She frowned and put a hand to her hair. "Wait, does my hair look bad?"

Jasmine scrutinized her. "It's okay, but it's been awhile. You should probably do something before summer really kicks in. The humidity will do nightmarish things to your curls."

"I suppose you're right. Can you fit me in for a trim?"

"Of course I can. You just hold on a few minutes, and we'll say goodbye to those split ends." Jasmine tousled her current customer's hair, giving it a lift and once-over before removing the black plastic apron clipped at the woman's neck. "You are all set, Miss Virginia."

The older woman touched her permed gray curls and smiled. "You always make me feel so young, Jasmine. I think I'll go dancing tonight. I didn't get a chance to dance at Jardin d'Amandes last weekend."

"That sounds lovely. Your husband will enjoy having you on his arm tonight."

The woman stood and walked to the front counter to check out. "We do need to reschedule another fund-raiser," she said as she opened her purse to retrieve her wallet. "As you know, we had to cut the evening short. Those poor youngsters won't make it to the competition at this rate."

"Yes, ma'am, I heard about it. Jillian, didn't you cater that event?" Jasmine called from the register.

"Yes, I did. I'm sorry, I don't think we met at the fund-raiser." She reached a hand out to the older woman. "I'm Jillian Green from The Chocolate Shoppe Bakery."

The woman offered a limp shake. "Virginia Porter. Charmed to meet you. So it was you who made those delicious desserts. You must make them again when we reschedule."

Porter? Jillian wondered if her husband was the man whose wallet had been stolen at the fund-raiser. "I would be honored. When you have a date, call the bakery and I'll put it on the calendar."

"Well, I do need to run it by the committee, of course."

"Of course." Jillian smiled. "Who else is on the committee?" She hoped she didn't sound too nosy.

"Oh, let me think. Richard Meyer, the wedding planner here

in town. He's a wonderful organizer. And Lisa Flint, who handles our printing needs."

"She must have printed those eye-catching posters," Jillian said. Lisa's shop, Print Worthy, was just across the street from the bakery, and she always did top-notch work.

"Yes, but do you know, they were designed by one of the members of the high school jazz band. Quite impressive for someone without any formal training, don't you think?"

Jillian felt a tinge of embarrassment that she'd critiqued the teen's artwork so harshly. "The artist certainly shows promise. Now, isn't Lucinda Atwood on the committee too? She was so generous to offer her home for the event."

"Oh, yes, Lucinda is the chairwoman of the arts commission and heads up the planning committee. She's the brains behind it all. We couldn't do it without her."

"Wasn't it her choice to hire the piano player? The one who killed that man?" Jillian hated publicly accusing Jeremiah when she knew in her heart he was innocent, but she figured it was a calculated risk to see if it would elicit much response from this woman.

Virginia's face drooped, and her mouth opened and closed like a fish out of water. "I really wouldn't know. Someone recommended him, I suppose. I need to be going. Jasmine, keep the change."

She practically ran from the salon, her block heels barely touching the floor in her escape. The bell jingled loudly as she burst through the door. Jillian watched her out the salon window. At the curb, the woman stopped, and a red sports car pulled to a screeching halt in front of her.

Was that her husband picking her up? Jillian expected her to climb in. The passenger side window rolled down, but Jillian couldn't make out the driver on the other side of the car. After a few moments, the window rolled back up and the car zoomed off, leaving the older woman standing stiff as a statue. She glanced around furtively. Her face was white as a sheet and bore a panicked expression. She hurried down the street and climbed into a luxury car, then screeched out of the spot and whipped the car around in a U-turn, racing off in the opposite direction of the red sports car.

Jillian was perplexed. What could the driver of the sports car have said to make her take off like that?

"You ready, Jillian?" Jasmine asked, shaking out a fresh apron.

Jillian left the window for the stylist's chair, but her mind remained on the street and the odd scene that had just taken place.

Who was that? And why would someone want to threaten a sweet old lady on the arts commission?

10

Saturday morning, Jillian rushed through her routine to roll the bread dough, whip the coconut macaroons, and melt the chocolate she needed to cover the cake pops that were currently chilling. Now she closed the lid on a box of perfect raspberry almond scones and was ready to take a break. She knew exactly where these were heading. After meeting Virginia Porter and speaking with Jeremiah, her next step was clear.

She needed to speak with Lucinda Atwood.

"The delivery van is loaded up and ready to go," Lenora announced, removing her apron. "I'll be back in a jiffy."

Instantly, Jillian saw her way clear to Lucinda's house. "Lenora, I have to run some errands, so why don't I do the deliveries today? You stay here and watch the shop with Bertie and Maggie."

"Are you sure, Jillian? I'm feeling like myself again today."

"I'm going out anyway." Jillian grabbed the keys from the cabinet drawer and was out the back door before Lenora could give a response.

As she climbed into the van, Jillian spotted the list of deliveries on the passenger seat. Her first stop was the senior center. She checked the clock on the dash to see it was nearly ten o'clock. With five deliveries on the schedule, she figured she would arrive at Lucinda's mansion by noon—earlier if she didn't get caught up in too much chitchat.

After shaking off a few questions about what had happened at the fund-raiser and several more overly personal inquiries into her relationship with Hunter, Jillian got out of the senior center and completed the rest of the deliveries fairly quickly.

Just before noon, she pulled the van up in front of the wrought iron gate outside Jardin d'Amandes. She had been in such a hurry the previous Saturday to get inside and prepare for the event that she hadn't really looked at the regal manor, so she took a moment to appreciate its beauty.

With its spotless white paint, the mansion gleamed like a beacon in the Georgia sun. Eight stately—and enormous—pillars lined an expansive porch, and black shutters punctuated the arched windows that dotted the facade. Expertly clipped topiaries were planted at regular intervals along the foundation in beds full of brilliantly colored annuals.

Just as Cornelia had said, a gigantic marble obelisk was stuck right in the center of the circular drive, the estate name proudly carved into its base. A depiction of an almond tree wrapped around the obelisk itself. Jillian thought of poor Glendon Powell, whose wife had left him after he'd failed to make a go of an almond orchard. *At least old Glendon didn't have to deal with a murder on his property.*

Jillian put the van in park and killed the engine. All along the quiet street, cars were parked beneath magnolia trees, the glossy green leaves casting shadows on the vehicles. She glanced in the rearview mirror and saw a familiar red sports car at the curb a few yards back.

Jillian wondered if it was the same car that had pulled up in front of the salon yesterday. Did it belong to Lucinda?

Jillian exited the van and approached the red car, peering through the darkened windows. She couldn't picture the old woman, who had needed assistance coming down her curved staircase the night of the party, driving this flashy coupe. Rolling her eyes at herself, Jillian also realized that Lucinda would most certainly park her own car securely on the gated estate.

So who owns it?

Deciding to shelve that question for now, Jillian grabbed the box of scones and got out of the van. She strode purposefully to the pedestrian gate, expecting to find an intercom system. Instead, she saw that the gate latch was halfway undone, and she lifted it the rest of the way with ease. She made her way up a pristine stone walkway toward the house, where it forked off toward either side of the mansion or up broad marble stairs to a black front door.

She climbed the steps, taking each one in slow trepidation. Suddenly, she wasn't so sure what she was doing here. Brushing off her nerves, she reached the top step and crossed the wide front porch to the door. She raised her hand to grasp the bronze knocker. But before she did, she was stopped in her tracks by the sound of voices coming from beyond the tall, perfectly trimmed hedges to the side of the porch.

She heard a woman's laugh, sounding youthful and carefree. A reply followed, too quietly for Jillian to make out what was said or by whom. She walked to the end of the porch. The shrubbery mostly blocked the view, but Jillian was able to make out the back of a blonde woman who definitely resembled Flannery Garland. When the figure turned to the side to give the person in front of her a hug, Jillian was sure it was Flannery—and she was hugging Lucinda. The two embraced for what seemed a long time, and Jillian slipped back into the shadows, unwilling to interrupt and in need of some time to reflect on the encounter.

When Flannery walked by, Jillian pressed back against the house. She watched Flannery leave through the gate and take a left out onto the sidewalk. From there, she lost sight of the young woman.

Jillian contemplated forgoing her visit to Lucinda to follow Flannery, but what would be the reason if she got caught? Right now, speaking to Lucinda made the most sense.

Jillian returned to the front door and reached for the knocker again. She let it drop against the metal plate, and the noise echoed around her with deep finality. Footsteps sounded inside the house, growing increasingly louder, and then the door opened.

"Did you forget something, my de—?" Lucinda startled at the sight of Jillian. She dropped her gaze to the bakery box in Jillian's hands, then took a step back with a nervous expression. "I'm sorry, I thought you were someone else. I'm really not up for meeting with guests right now. If you'll excuse me."

Before Lucinda could seal the door, Jillian pushed the box forward. "I'm Jillian Green. You hired me to cater the fund-raiser last week."

The door paused. "Oh, forgive me, I didn't recognize you." Lucinda placed an aged hand on her chest. "What with that nice fund-raiser I threw turning into a complete nightmare, my mind and memory are clouded." Her eyes misted up and she dropped her anguished face to shield it from Jillian.

"I'm sorry to bother you, but I heard from someone on the committee that the fund-raiser will be rescheduled."

"Yes, of course. The children are depending on us. But it's hard to say when. There's too much pain right now."

"You were close to the deceased?"

At first she thought the woman would refuse to answer, but then she said tightly, "If you'll excuse me. I am just too distraught over bringing that vile crook to Moss Hollow."

"I'm assuming you mean Jeremiah Davis?"

"Don't say that name in my presence," Lucinda said sharply.

"I'm sorry, but you did hire him, correct?" Jillian positioned herself so that the box of scones would slow the door if Lucinda shut it on her. "How did you discover him? He really is a talented man."

"Yes, making it all the more shameful to see it end this way for him." Lucinda frowned and seemed genuinely distraught, but Jillian wasn't sure if it was over Jeremiah's circumstances or something else. She glanced beyond Jillian toward the street and, in a flash, pushed the door closed on the box, bending its sides. She glared at the box and then at Jillian. "You really should go now."

"Of, course, I'm sorry. I only wanted to stop by and give you a gift since you didn't get to taste the scones you requested. We do hope you will consider us again for another function." Jillian passed the box through the narrow opening in the door.

Lucinda took it and slammed the door without a response, the painted wood coming within an inch of Jillian's nose.

"I guess I had that coming," she mumbled. She tried to sort through the thoughts ricocheting around in her skull as she made her way back to the delivery van. Flannery had sounded happy and bubbly—not exactly the behavior one would expect from a woman who just lost her fiancé. But maybe that was just her personality. She was a beauty queen, after all.

And then there was Lucinda. Based on her words at the fund-raiser and what Jillian had just witnessed, the wealthy woman seemed to think of Flannery almost as a daughter. Was it possible that she had discovered Sterling wasn't who he said he was and had hired someone to kill him? Sparing Flannery the heartache of marrying the wrong man could easily be a motive for murder—for the right person, anyway.

Jillian was beginning to develop a killer headache when she unlocked the van and started to climb in, but something out of place caught her eye. Something had changed since she had left the street before.

The red sports car was gone from its parking spot. Driven off by Flannery, no doubt.

A tune wiggled its way into Jillian's head, and she caught herself humming it and then singing it as she fired up the van and took off down the magnolia-lined street.

"I wonder who's kissing her now . . . I wonder who's looking into her eyes, breathing sighs, telling lies . . ." The song stayed with

Jillian the entire way back to the shop. The pianist at Ken's Piano Bar had been telling her something about Flannery, she was certain. The question was, what did the pageant beauty's new flame have to do with the murder of Bo Tyler and the fact that there was an innocent man in jail likely to be indicted for it?

What if they were all in on it? The thought hit Jillian like an anvil. Suddenly Bo Tyler's murder switched from a heated battle of scammers to something so potentially sinister and calculated that Jillian shot a backward glance in her rearview mirror, reflexively checking for another tailgater.

Stick to baking or else.

The warning came flooding back, renewing her urge to get back to the relative safety of The Chocolate Shoppe. As much as she wanted to help free Jeremiah, Jillian wasn't sure she was up for finding out what "or else" meant.

"You've been awfully quiet this weekend, Jillian. And you hightailed it out of church so fast this morning, I thought your skirt was on fire." Bertie's words came seemingly out of nowhere, but Jillian could feel her grandmother's piercing gaze from across the bakery kitchen. Bertie had just arrived for the Sweetie Pies meeting, but Jillian had been there for hours already, avoiding reality—and overanalyzing it at the same time—through baking.

"Can't a girl just dive into her work?" Jillian put a sheet of double-chocolate cookies into the oven and set the timer.

Bertie arched an eyebrow toward the ceiling. "In a word? No. You'd best tell me what's the matter, young lady. Is there trouble with you and Hunter?"

"No, we're fine." Jillian slapped the magnetic timer onto the oven door with more force than was necessary, then released a resigned sigh. If anyone could offer her advice, it was Bertie. "I think I'm in over my head. I set out to make sure a killer stayed behind bars, but in doing so, I realized he's likely not the killer. Only now that I am getting closer to finding out who put that knife in Bo Tyler's back, I'm realizing I might be attempting to take on two pillars of Moss Hollow society."

"Which two?"

"Lucinda Atwood and Flannery Garland."

Bertie let out a slow whistle. "You can't be serious. Those women wouldn't get blood on their hands. It might stain their Chanel."

"I know. But that's precisely what's scaring me. There must be a third person involved with them. Someone with the muscle to kill." Jillian hesitated, then decided that she should confess. "Someone who left a note on the front door of Belle Haven the other night, telling me to stick to baking."

Bertie scoped out the stuffed cooling racks. "So that explains the silent treatment. You've taken them up on their request."

"It was more of a threat, really. The note ended with an 'or else.'"

"And what did Gooder say about the note?"

Jillian cleared her throat and focused on cleaning her hands instead of Bertie's question dangling in the air between them. "Well, actually, you see—"

"You haven't told him," Bertie guessed.

Jillian shook her head.

Bertie clucked her tongue. "Good thing the other Sweetie Pies will be here shortly. You can unburden yourself on Laura Lee and she can tell you, in a professional capacity, to can it with the so-called investigating. I'll never forgive you if you get yourself killed."

A short while later, the front of the bakery had three tables pushed together with a pitcher of sweet tea and a tray of cookies at the ready. All of the Sweetie Pies except Wanda Jean, who had a summer cold, and Maudie, whose husband had just had knee surgery, had arrived and were greeting each other warmly.

Savannah approached Jillian and gave her a concerned frown. "Something bothering you?"

Jillian shrugged, but before she could say anything, Bertie made an announcement. "Girls, I believe Jillian would like to get something off her chest."

Subtle, Bertie. "I suppose I would. Please, sit." Jillian waved to the chairs. "I don't know how you'll feel about what I'm going to say."

"Does this have something to do with why you've been in the kitchen every waking hour this weekend?" Lenora asked.

"I've wondered about that too," Savannah said. "I thought you were avoiding me when you didn't respond to my e-mail about shopping for a maid-of-honor dress. I was starting to worry you didn't like the color I picked."

Jillian could tell Savannah was trying to make a joke, but it didn't do much to assuage her nerves. "No, it's not that at all."

When the Sweetie Pies had taken their seats, Jillian noticed no one reached for drinks or cookies. All eyes were on her. She took a deep breath. No need to draw this out.

"I think I've uncovered who is responsible for the murder of Sterling Macon, aka Bo Tyler." She flitted a glance at Laura Lee. "I have reason to believe that Lucinda Atwood and Flannery Garland are involved."

Voices erupted from around the table, the consensus being that Jillian had lost her marbles. Lucinda was a kind and generous pillar of the community, always willing to open her pocketbook for a cause. And Flannery was a local celebrity who visited sick children in the hospital and wore a smile at local grand openings.

Jillian held up a hand to stop them. "I'm not saying they killed the man. I'm just saying they know more than they are letting on." She recounted the reasons she had to suspect the women, then reached into her purse and pulled out the note that had been taped to her front door. "And the other day, I received this note on the front door at Belle Haven. It had to be from someone who knew where I had been."

"And where was that?" Laura Lee asked, sounding much more like a sheriff's deputy than a Sweetie Pie.

"Well, I'm sure it's no secret in the sheriff's department, but I went to visit Jeremiah Davis in jail."

The room erupted into chatter again, a chorus of "What were you thinking?" and "Why would you do a fool thing like that?" clashing with the sweet-smelling air.

Jillian shushed them and continued. "But it wasn't until I

went to Jeremiah's hometown to do a little fact-finding mission on him that I came home to Belle Haven to find this note taped to my front door."

Cornelia stood up so fast her chair's legs scraped loudly through the shop. "Why, forevermore! Another miscreant was lurking around our property and came as close as the front door without our knowing? I knew Raymond was trying to tell us something when he knocked over that plant." She put a hand to her face. "Jillian, you should have told us immediately."

"I'm sorry, Cornelia. You're right. I should have."

Laura Lee cleared her throat. "You should have told the sheriff's office right away. Now, I'm going to ask you to hand over the note."

Annalise rested a hand on Jillian's arm and gave her a comforting squeeze. "Laura Lee, do you think you can track down whoever wrote that thing?"

"I'll test it, even though it's unlikely we'll find anything. Most people know to wear gloves these days. But don't worry. We'll probably find out who wrote this when we get the full explanation for the strange things that have been happening lately." Laura Lee had pulled on a pair of latex gloves and was already placing the note in a plastic bag. The woman came prepared. "But I have to ask you, Jillian: Why does this matter so much to you? You received a threatening note and you still went out to Lucinda's home to dig up more information?"

Jillian frowned. "I know the sheriff's department is focusing efforts on finding evidence that points to Jeremiah Davis as the killer—"

"The sheriff's office is focusing efforts on finding evidence that points to the killer, period," Laura Lee interrupted tersely, then her face softened. "Jillian, you should know we would never ignore due process just because a suspect has a list of priors."

"I didn't mean to imply that, Laura Lee," Jillian said. "It's just that, even though I might have thought him guilty at one time,

I don't believe he's a murderer anymore. After meeting with him a second time—"

"A second time!" Cornelia screeched.

Jillian flinched but held her ground. "Yes, and I'm so glad I did. I honestly don't understand why he's still in jail as it is. He's not being charged with murder to my knowledge. Does the sheriff have something more on him than finding the wallet in his car, Laura Lee?"

The deputy paused and seemed to be sizing her up. Finally she said, "Well, I suppose you'd find out anyway if you asked the right people. Jeremiah can't make bail, which isn't surprising considering his background. And the bail was set especially high in his case."

"Why? That doesn't seem fair," Annalise objected.

"Turns out Alton Porter didn't just have a license and a few twenty-dollar bills in his wallet. He's a big gambler, and he always keeps a 1933 Indian Head Gold Eagle coin with him for luck. It's valued at hundreds of thousands of dollars."

Gasps met Laura Lee's revelation, and the room erupted in chatter. Josi, the town's reference librarian, said, "I knew Mr. Porter was a numismatist because he comes into the library for books all the time, but I didn't realize he owned anything that valuable."

Jillian had a cold feeling in her bones. "So does that mean Jeremiah is being held on grand larceny?"

Laura Lee shrugged. "Something like that."

"He doesn't deserve that," Jillian protested. "You should have seen his face when I told him what I learned about Bo Tyler. Jeremiah was genuinely worried for my safety. He asked me to step back and forget about him and this whole murder case."

"As you should," Lenora said. "You're going to get yourself into more mess than you know what to do with, child."

I think that's already happened, Jillian thought, but kept it to herself.

"Jeremiah Davis is not what he seems," Laura Lee said. "He knows how to prey on innocent people and tell them what they need to hear to trust him. Then he—" She stopped short.

"He scams them," Jillian finished for her. "That may have been the case for him before, but I really don't believe it is in this situation. He told me about a con Bo Tyler was working on an elderly widow. It was Jeremiah who stepped in to alert the victim, saving her from being swindled. That widow was Lucinda. If anyone would want Bo dead, it would be her."

Cornelia clasped her hands together. "Wait. If Lucinda was the widow Bo Tyler marked, and Jeremiah saved her from losing her money, perhaps she hired Jeremiah to kill the man."

"No." Jillian couldn't let that line of thinking continue. "Jeremiah did not kill anyone. He's not a killer."

"How can you be so sure?" Lenora asked.

Jillian gave her friends a level gaze. "I've seen where he's from. I've seen the people whose lives he's touched in a good way, like a young boy and Jeremiah's elderly neighbor. They care about Jeremiah." Jillian shook her head, adamant about her stance. "Jeremiah Davis has had to fight for his life. But I don't think he'd kill for it."

Laura Lee stood. "I'm going to take this note in to process it. But Jillian"—she met Jillian's gaze squarely—"please leave the investigating to the authorities. You may have stumbled onto something dangerous here. I'd hate to see you get hurt."

"So you believe me? You believe Jeremiah didn't do this and the real killer is still out there somewhere?"

"That's not what I said at all. I think there may be others involved in the scam."

"What scam?"

"The scam to get Jeremiah Davis off. I'm sorry to say this, but there's a good chance that man is conning you right now."

Disheartened at the sour turn the Sweetie Pies meeting had taken, Jillian had spent the rest of Sunday trying to read a book, but she couldn't concentrate. Her mind insisted on wandering over the facts at hand. Was she giving Jeremiah too much credit? Was she not giving Flannery and Lucinda enough? The answers still eluded her as she arrived at the bakery Monday morning and started her day.

Midmorning, she was just refilling pastries in the front display case when Annalise walked in. Her brown eyes flashed friendliness as she greeted Jillian. "I think I left my sunglasses here after the meeting yesterday," she said. "They're in a green case. Did you find it anywhere?"

Jillian nodded. "Maggie found it this morning when she was opening. It's right here." She grabbed the case from next to the cash register and handed it to Annalise.

"Thanks, Jillian. Byron would have a cow if I lost these. Normally he wouldn't care a whit, but he's had to work a lot of late hours at the bank lately since they've merged with the credit union. He's like a bear with a sore tooth."

"Sounds like it's putting a real strain on your relationship."

"A bit, but I know it won't last. They should be finished with the transition soon, and then I'll have my sweet Byron back." Annalise gave a wan smile, then her eyes brightened. "I've been thinking about what you said yesterday. You know, about Flannery Garland being involved in that man's death."

"And?" Jillian's ears perked up at the prospect of a new lead.

"You might consider talking to Anita Coleman."

"The president of the Nathan County Junior League?" Jillian knit her brows. "Why her?"

"Her daughter, Paige, did pageants with Flannery." Annalise gave a conspiratorial wink. "Or I should say, against Flannery. They were each other's main competition for the local pageants, and from what I recall, Flannery usually won. Anita's husband works with Byron at the bank, so I heard a lot about it."

"I'm sure Paige—and her mother—didn't appreciate that."

"Certainly not. And from what Byron has said, Brock Coleman has always held a bit of a grudge against Earle Garland for doing his banking in Atlanta instead of locally."

"Sounds like a recipe for resentment to me," Jillian said.

Annalise nodded. "Anyway, if you want insight into Flannery, it'd be a place to start."

"Thanks, Annalise." Jillian flashed a grateful smile.

"No, thank you," Annalise said, holding up her sunglasses case before putting it in her purse. "This is my favorite pair."

Jillian started to reply, but she heard one of her timers going off in the kitchen. "Sorry, gotta run. Thanks for the tip, though."

"No problem," Annalise said. "Good luck with everything."

Work had kept Hunter busy all weekend, so Jillian had told herself it would be rude to interrupt him. However, she knew that she should tell him that she'd been back to the jail sooner rather than later—before Bertie beat her to it again. *Not to mention that I've been running around town accusing rich widows of hiring assassins.* She needed his help sorting through this mess of a case. Of course, she'd also missed him while he'd been tied up at the funeral home, but she was eager to get his input on what she'd learned.

The front door to the sprawling Victorian that housed the mortuary creaked with a bit of the same trepidation that she felt. Entering the welcoming, serene foyer, Jillian glanced around for any sign of life. Hunter's Lexus was the lone vehicle in the parking lot, aside from the hearse, so she knew she wasn't interrupting a visitation.

"Hello?" Jillian called down the hall. She moved past a round table that held a lovely vase of flowers. "Is anyone here?"

No response came, so Jillian continued down to Hunter's office. She rapped on the dark oak door, but she still didn't get an answer. If he wasn't in his office, she could think of only one other place he'd be. He must be in his other office—the embalming room.

At that thought, Jillian decided it probably wasn't a good time for a visit. Her news could wait until later, as she had no desire to try to talk to him over any corpses, especially if he had Bo back there. She shuddered and retreated back down the hall and had her hand on the front doorknob when a vaguely familiar voice stopped her in her tracks.

"Jillian?"

She did an about-face. "Hi. Val, right?"

"In the flesh," the woman said brightly. She was about fifty and had spiky red hair tinged with purple. She wore tight black jeans and a red top, and she offered Jillian a hand covered in silver rings. "Nice to meet you. The boss talks about you all the time."

Jillian shook Val's hand. "I didn't see any other cars in the lot."

"My struts went out on me." Val shrugged. "At least it was a nice day for a walk."

"Would you like a ride home?" Jillian offered. "I'd be happy to drive you."

"Nah," Val said as Hunter joined them in the foyer, an expression of pleasant surprise on his face. The substitute assistant eyed both Hunter and Jillian with a knowing sparkle lighting up her heavily made-up face. "I don't want to get in the way of whatever date night you two lovebirds have planned."

"We don't have any plans that I know of," Hunter said. "Did I forget something, Jillian?"

"No, but I have a few things I wanted to talk over with you. Nothing that can't wait if you want a ride, Val, or if you're too busy, Hunter."

"I need a break, and you're a nice one," he told her warmly.

"I'm good," Val said. "These boots were made for walking." She clicked her leather-covered heels together, then bustled out of the funeral home with a wave. "Don't you two do anything I wouldn't do."

Hunter laughed. "No worries there. We're pretty tame."

"I'm sorry for just showing up without calling or anything," Jillian said after the door was shut behind Val.

"I'm not." He leaned close and placed a kiss on her cheek. "It's nice to see you."

"It's nice to see you too." She pulled away, resolved not to wait any longer. "But this visit is more business than pleasure."

"Let me guess," Hunter said. "This involves Jeremiah Davis?"

Jillian nodded.

"I'm guessing our brains will work better if we discuss it over a glass of sweet tea. Come on to the kitchen." He took her hand and led her down the hall to the funeral home's large white kitchen. A small island rested in the center of the room, and two barstools were pulled up under its black granite countertop. Jillian hopped onto a stool as Hunter prepared their drinks. He retrieved a pitcher of sweet tea from the refrigerator, then brought down two glasses from the cabinet near the sink and filled them. He added a lemon wedge to each before bringing them over to the island and sitting on the other stool.

For a moment, Jillian enjoyed the sense of domesticity the scene held. She drank deeply, not realizing until that moment how thirsty she'd been. "That's good," she told him.

Hunter was not to be deterred. "Talk to me, Jillian. Has something happened?"

"I think Val is going to be disappointed when you tell her how unromantic tonight is looking right now."

"Don't worry about Val," Hunter said with a grin as he held up his glass in a salute. "I'll tell her we talked late into the night over drinks. About—I don't know—flowers and stars and such. I won't mention anything about murder."

Jillian laughed. "I wish I could hear the story you'll tell. I'm pretty sure it's going to be a real humdinger."

"You can help me make it up later. Now what's on your mind?"

She took a deep breath and blurted out, "Do you think Jeremiah Davis is scamming me?"

Hunter's smile evaporated into a confused expression. "Why do you ask that?"

"Laura Lee thinks he is."

"I feel like you started this conversation in the middle," Hunter said. "Why don't you back up and start at the beginning."

"Okay. I went to see Jeremiah again. I wanted to ask him about Bo Tyler. And don't worry. There were at least a dozen guards in the room, and they had us talking through a cement wall, so I wasn't in a bit of danger."

Hunter couldn't help a laugh. "Now who's telling whoppers? Anyway, what did you find out?"

"Turns out Jeremiah saved Lucinda Atwood from being scammed by Sterling, or Bo, or whoever he was."

"And?"

"And I feel like that'd be a reasonable motive for Lucinda to hire someone to kill him."

"You don't actually believe she'd pay an assassin to take revenge, do you?" Hunter raised an eyebrow.

"It seems more likely than Jeremiah killing him for no good reason."

"I'm guessing this theory is why Laura Lee told you she thinks Jeremiah is scamming you." Hunter grabbed her glass and took it and his own to the counter to refill them.

"Apparently it's easier to believe one criminal could kill another instead of a rich old lady being behind it all."

"Laura Lee is a sheriff's deputy. She's literally trained to detect criminal activity."

"Maybe, but something just doesn't add up." Jillian hesitated. "Besides, there's something else that makes me believe that Jeremiah isn't behind all this. He couldn't exactly send a threatening note from jail."

Hunter came back with their full glasses, and there was unmistakable worry in his eyes as he said, "What kind of threatening note are we talking about here?"

"The kind that says 'Stick to baking or else' and gets taped to the front door of Belle Haven." She tried to sound offhand about it. "I got it the same night after we went to Beech Brook. I've already given it to Laura Lee."

"Whoever delivered that note doesn't seem to know you very well. There's no way you'll just stick to baking if someone needs your help." He reached over and took her hand. "It's one of my favorite things about you, if I'm being honest."

"I mean, I tried to stay out of it. I can't help it if my gut instinct is telling me everyone thinks the wrong man killed Sterling—er, Bo. Sure, Jeremiah isn't perfect—far from it, even according to himself—but having a rap sheet isn't enough evidence, especially when that rap sheet has no record of violence. He made it sound like there are powerful forces at work here."

"It seems like things started to escalate after we went to Beech Brook," Hunter said thoughtfully. "That car following us on the highway, then the threat." He looked down and took a deep breath, then met her gaze. "I'm not about to ask you to stop. I know you won't. But please keep the police—and me—in the loop. Let us help you, and please don't take any unnecessary risks. You know your safety is what's most important to me. When you put yourself in danger to help someone else, somebody's got to watch out for you."

Jillian smiled and kissed his cheek. "When you put it like that, it sounds almost romantic."

Hunter smiled. "Val would be proud."

Annalise's recommendation to contact Anita Coleman had slipped to the back of Jillian's mind, so she hadn't done anything about it. But as it turned out, she didn't have to. Midmorning on Tuesday, the bakery phone rang, and Jillian, who had just slid a pan of brownies in the oven, went to answer it. "Chocolate Shoppe Bakery, Jillian speaking. What can we do for you today?"

"Is this the bakery that catered the Sweet Sounds fund-raiser?" the caller asked.

"It is," Jillian answered, hoping it wasn't someone looking for gossip about the murder. They'd had their share of those calls, e-mails, and drop-ins the last week, and she wasn't sure she could take much more.

"This is Anita Coleman, and I was there that evening. The murder business was unfortunate and all, but really, dear, your desserts were wonderful."

"Thank you. We always like hearing from people who enjoy what we make."

"Do you happen to do wedding cakes?"

"Of course," Jillian said enthusiastically, then wondered what Anita Coleman needed with a wedding cake when she was married to Byron Reed's coworker.

"My daughter, Paige, is getting married this fall and we were going to go with a bakery in Atlanta, but I'm quite convinced that you folks are the ones for the job, and I'd rather keep it local anyway. I mean, really, if those petits fours were anything to go by, your cakes must be simply divine."

Jillian smiled, thinking she'd need to pass along the compliment to the Sweetie Pies at their next meeting. "Does Paige have a particular style or design in mind? We can make just about any shape, and decorate it however she wants."

Mrs. Coleman's sigh was clearly audible through the phone. "I'm afraid Paige won't have much say in the matter. She's finishing up her master's degree at the university and won't be done until the week before the wedding. She doesn't need to be driving the hour each way every time I get an idea in my head."

"Would you like me to e-mail her our portfolio?"

"Oh, no, dear, that won't do. I wouldn't want to distract her from her studies. Besides, she has given me carte blanche to make choices as I see fit. Whoever holds the purse strings holds the power, and all."

Jillian was a little surprised at the woman's declaration, but figured she ought to go along with it. If she was the president of the Junior League, she could easily lead to much more business from Moss Hollow's ladies-who-lunch crowd. "I understand. Would you like me to e-mail the portfolio to you?"

"Do you have anything real? I mean, computer pictures are fine and all, but I would prefer something I can get my hands on."

Jillian smiled. "I know a lot of people who feel the same way. We have an album here with photos of all of our cakes."

Before Jillian could recommend a time for Mrs. Coleman to stop by the bakery and see the album, the woman said, "Splendid. When can you come over?"

"You mean bring it to your home?"

"Is that a problem?"

"No—"

"Good, then, how is this afternoon? I have a nail appointment at three, but otherwise, I am fairly available."

Jillian glanced at the to-do list posted near the phone and realized that her extra work baking the previous weekend had been a blessing. "How's two o'clock? I'll even bring a few petits fours."

At the appointed time, Jillian arrived on the doorstep of the Colemans' stately brick Georgian. The home was nowhere near as large as Jardin d'Amandes, but it had a classic charm all its own. She balanced a box of petits fours and the photo album in one hand and rang the bell with the other.

Mrs. Coleman opened the door in a cloud of expensive perfume. Her bubblegum-pink lipstick matched her cashmere cardigan, and large pearls gleamed amid the woman's perfect blonde locks. "Come in, dear. Is that the petits fours?" Not waiting for a response, she took the box from Jillian's outstretched hand and led the way into a foyer wallpapered in a floral pattern. "Our sitting room is being redecorated, so I'm afraid we'll have to settle for the formal dining room. Please pardon the mess."

Jillian saw no signs of mess in the pristine home, which looked as though it hadn't seen a cobweb or a dust bunny in its hundred or so years. "You have a lovely home, Mrs. Coleman."

"It's not as grand as Belle Haven, I'm afraid, but we make do."

Somewhat surprised that Mrs. Coleman knew where she lived, Jillian stumbled over her answer. "No, but much cleaner."

Mrs. Coleman laughed politely as they entered the dining room. "Do have a seat."

"Thank you." Jillian placed the album on a glossy cherrywood tabletop that she guessed to be either a genuine antique or a very good reproduction. She settled into a chair with an ornately carved back and a seat upholstered in burgundy damask, then gazed appreciatively at the room's decor. The Asian-inspired silk wallpaper depicted dark-bronze bamboo on a gold background, and cream-colored dentil molding lined the ceiling. She wondered just how many crystals were woven into the sparkling chandelier over her head.

Perched in her own chair beside Jillian, Mrs. Coleman sat ramrod straight, a smile painted on her face. Jillian wondered if she had her own history of competing in beauty pageants.

"Here's the album I mentioned," Jillian said, passing the book to Mrs. Coleman.

Seemingly reluctant to set the still-tied box of petits fours aside, Mrs. Coleman accepted the book and made space for it on the table. As she leafed through it, she murmured polite comments at photos she liked and, Jillian assumed, said nothing about the ones she didn't. *The essential Miss Manners.*

"Can you tell me a bit about what kind of wedding this will be?" Jillian asked.

"It'll be in December at the country club. We've chosen pink as the main color, with some metallic accents." Mrs. Coleman continued to leaf through the album. "This one with the flowers is nice. Are they real?"

Jillian leaned over to study the photo. "Yes, they're real. We can work with your florist if that's something you'd like. Or Paige and her groom would like."

"Hmm. I'd really like something more . . . special. Do you understand my meaning?"

Jillian smiled. "I think I do. In fact, I've been working on something new lately that just might be what you're looking for." She pulled out her phone and brought up the photo gallery. She'd taken a few photos of her latest attempt at sugared magnolias, a batch that was finally close to what she had imagined for so long. "If you like them, Paige could be the first bride to have them on her cake."

Mrs. Coleman's eyes seemed to light up as she accepted Jillian's phone and gazed at the image on the screen. "Yes, these are lovely. What are they?"

"Sugared magnolias, molded from gum paste and hand-painted."

"I think they're just perfect. I love them." Mrs. Coleman glanced up from the phone and seemed to catch herself. "And Paige will adore them too, no doubt."

"I'm so glad," Jillian said. "Speaking of Paige, did I hear correctly that she competed in pageants when she was younger?"

"Oh yes, she did. She was exquisite." Mrs. Coleman's eyes danced at the memory. "Wait just a moment." She left the room briefly and returned with her own album. "Here's her memory book. She was such a treasure."

Jillian smiled politely as she accepted the book and opened it. A teenage girl who was a forty-years-younger version of Anita Coleman smiled from the front page, a small tiara glittering on her head. "She's a real beauty. You must be so proud."

"Oh, certainly. She competed in so many pageants, it was hard to keep track."

Jillian remembered what Annalise had said about Flannery often besting Paige, so she didn't ask if the girl had won any titles. She leafed through pages until she caught sight of a familiar face—well, half a face, anyway. The photo, a candid backstage shot of several girls, appeared to have been cropped creatively to remove as much of the person as possible. "Is that Flannery?" Jillian asked.

"Who?" Mrs. Coleman raised her perfectly plucked eyebrows.

"Flannery Garland?" If Mrs. Coleman was pretending not to know her, the rivalry must have cut deeper than Annalise had even known.

"Oh. Yes. That's her."

"Were the girls close?" Jillian wondered how much Mrs. Coleman would be willing to share, if anything.

"No, I wouldn't say that. Although Flannery certainly coveted so much of what our sweet Paige had."

"What makes you say that?"

"Oh, she often cut her hair the same or chose a competition dress in a similar color. Quite flattering, really."

"I see."

"Poor girl really started to lose her way after her mother passed. Although, God rest her soul, Blanche Garland wasn't the easiest woman to . . . engage with."

"How do you mean Flannery lost her way?" Jillian asked.

"Well, after Blanche died, Flannery didn't seem to care whose heart she broke. There never seemed to be enough boys for her to date. She even stole my Paige's young man right out from under her. Nasty business, really."

Jillian could feel some hostility starting to crack Mrs. Coleman's poise, so she tried to right the ship. "Well, no harm done, right? Paige is going to be married. And her wedding will be lovely, especially with you in charge."

"It certainly will. It'll be the wedding of the year now that Flannery's engagement has ended."

"As long as Paige is happy, that's what matters." Jillian could sense that it was nearing time for her to leave.

Anita's mouth curved into a smile that seemed almost vicious. "Living well is the best revenge, isn't it?"

"And then I figured it would be best if I left. She seemed to be getting a little worked up, and I think I got about as much as I could have from her," Jillian told Savannah as she took her cell phone off hands-free mode and got out of her car. "She kept the petits fours, so I hope she'll call back and order the cake."

"Sounds like an interesting visit," Savannah said. "I don't know them well, but from what I hear, the Colemans have always been what you might call social climbers."

"Yeah, I got that impression." Jillian fished her key out of her purse, unlocked Belle Haven's front door, and stepped inside. "I also got the distinct impression that there's serious bad blood between them and Flanner—ouch!"

After closing the door, Jillian had turned and slammed her hip into something solid. The sudden jolt sent her phone clattering to the ground a few feet away.

"Jillian? What happened?" Savannah's voice emanated from the phone.

Jillian clutched her throbbing hip, then recovered her phone. "Sorry. Just ran into something . . . unexpected in the foyer." She pivoted to see what had stood in her way. "And it's a piano. What the—Cornelia!"

"I better let you go so you can sort that out," Savannah said with a chuckle.

"Talk to you later," Jillian said, then disconnected the call.

Cornelia appeared, the serenity in her face in direct opposition to Jillian's ruffled appearance. For some reason, this irritated Jillian even more, especially when Cornelia said calmly, "There's no need to holler, Jillian."

"Aunt Cornelia, what is that?" Jillian jabbed a finger at the upright piano resting next to the front door. "And why is it in our foyer?"

"I told you I was going to have the piano brought down from the attic, didn't I?"

"Yes, but I didn't think you were serious." *Though I suppose I should know better by now.*

Cornelia made a dismissive gesture as she walked over to the instrument. "Just think, dear. How wonderful will it be to have some music echoing through our halls? The haint will love it, I'm certain. It'll be a tribute to her grand old days. You know, with the parties she used to host and all." Cornelia maintained that Belle Haven was haunted by the ghost of Virginia Belle, the wife of the Captain Hoyt Belle, who had built the mansion before the Civil War. She pressed a few of the keys whimsically, but all the piano emitted was dissonant noise.

Jillian rubbed her sore hip. The cacophonous chord had reminded her uncomfortably of the discordant and seemingly conflicting bits of information she had about who had killed Bo Tyler. Would she ever be able to arrange them into a meaningful song?

14

On Wednesday afternoon, Jillian set out for the Avondale mansion, home of the Garland family. She knew that unless she spoke to Flannery herself, she wouldn't be able to get rid of the idea that the pageant queen was capable of murder.

The stately Greek Revival loomed ahead as she steered her Prius through the open gate and up the driveway. Not quite as large as Jardin d'Amandes, the brick mansion was still an impressive sight with its thick pillars and towering portico. Ahead of her, a black limousine rested at the base of the front steps, presided over by twin lion sculptures guarding the home.

Glancing around for the chauffeur or his passenger, Jillian didn't see any sign of life. In fact, all she saw was acre after acre of rural land. She parked the Prius behind the limousine and steeled herself for whatever happened next. She climbed the steps and rang the doorbell, which played two booming notes that vibrated in the pit of her stomach. Their deep tone felt like harbingers of doom rather than welcome. When no one answered, she hesitated to ring it again.

Where is everyone?

No chauffeur, no butler to answer the door. There had to be a maid or two inside somewhere. A place this size would need a whole entourage to keep it going.

She turned and assessed her surroundings. Remembering Lucinda's neatly trimmed topiaries, she frowned a little at the lopsided hedges, unevenly cut grass, and untended flower beds that made up the landscaping at Avondale.

Jillian rubbed her fingers together, preparing to ring the

formidable doorbell again. She cringed and reached for the round button, but before she touched it, the front door was yanked wide, revealing the elderly gentleman who had escorted Lucinda Atwood down the stairs at the fund-raiser. Only that man had been tidied up in an expensive tuxedo without a hair out of place. This version's thinning hair protruded wildly from his head, and his eyes were encircled with bags and darkness. Jillian knew Earle Garland had seen better days, because she had witnessed it firsthand just days ago.

What had happened to Earle to leave him in such disarray?

"Mr. Garland?" Jillian asked. At his blank expression, she continued. "I'm Jillian Green from The Chocolate Shoppe Bakery in town. I catered the Sweet Sounds fund-raiser."

The man squinted as though her words were spoken in a different language.

"I was wondering if I could speak to your daughter, Flannery. I have some information about her fiancé."

The man stared wildly around over Jillian's shoulders. He swallowed convulsively. "You need to go. Now." He moved to close the door.

Jillian put up a hand to stop it. "Please, Mr. Garland, is she here?"

"No," he said with an irritated glance at her hand. "And you shouldn't be either." He looked past her again, this time searching to his left. The move revealed a bloody gash below his ear, and it appeared to be a recent wound made by something sharp.

Jillian put her hand on the door to keep it from closing. "Mr. Garland, you're bleeding. Are you all right?"

He moved back into the shadows. "I'm fine." He reached to cover the cut. "My daughter's fiancé . . . he's a little rough around the edges."

"Her fiancé? But I thought her fiancé was dead."

The door slammed instantly.

"Wait, Mr. Garland!" Jillian didn't hesitate to ring the horrible doorbell again and again. She had more questions now than ever. She had been referring to Bo Tyler, but Earle Garland must have been talking about another man altogether—a man who was rough around the edges. *Rougher than Bo Tyler?* Whoever it was, he didn't seem to think hitting an elderly man was out of the question. Flannery's new fiancé was the one who was kissing her now, and apparently he was violent.

But who was it? Another con man? Was he from Moss Hollow? How had Flannery met him? Had he killed Bo Tyler to get him out of the picture so he could move in on Flannery? Had she been in on the plan? Or was Flannery setting herself up to be his next victim?

Endless questions had Jillian's head spinning. At her Prius, she leaned back against the driver's door and stood a moment, her thoughts whirring in confusion. Her surroundings slowly came into focus. The rolling hills stretched far and wide. The mossy trees that bordered the perimeter out in the distance seemed peaceful, until she realized not another home existed for miles.

The hair on Jillian's neck stood up and sent a shiver down her spine.

Her cell phone rang. She pulled it out and answered it with an absentminded, "Hello?"

"Jillian, it's Bertie."

Jillian offered a half-hearted acknowledgment as her unease crept back in. She perused the area in a slow circle. Something felt off. It was as though someone watched her.

"Jillian?" Bertie spoke louder. "Can you hear me?"

"Yes, I can. I'm at Avondale. It's a beautiful place."

"Why are you acting strangely? Are you hurt?"

"No." Jillian glanced at the windows of the house. They

stretched from floor to ceiling, with dark draperies blocking the sunlight and view inside.

Then one drapery moved.

Someone *was* watching her.

It could have been Earle Garland watching her leave, but this felt different, more sinister than an old man rushing her off.

"Jillian, you need to come back to the shop. Someone is here to see you."

Jillian stared at the window in trepidation. "Me?" she asked absently, not really concerned with a visitor at the bakery. Still, she asked, "Who is it? Hunter?" *I wish Hunter was with me now.*

"No, not quite," Bertie replied. "He says you promised him some cookies."

"He?" Now her interest piqued. "Does *he* have a name?"

"Don't know, but he can't be older than eleven or twelve. Hard to tell with his hair in his face. He sure does like your cookies, though."

Paulie.

Jillian yanked her car door open. "I'll be right there."

Jillian made it back to the bakery in record time. She burst through the front door to find Paulie sitting at a bistro table with a heaping pile of chocolate chip cookies, his filthy green baseball cap beside them. *Bertie must really love that.* Jillian glanced Bertie's way, but if her grandmother cared about the dirty cap on the table, she didn't let on. In fact, she had never looked more grandmotherly as she poured Paulie a tall glass of milk to go with his cookies, a beaming smile on her face.

Bertie barely glanced Jillian's way when she said, "Welcome back, Jillian. We were just getting acquainted with your friend. He finally told us his name. Seems he only gives out information if the payment is high enough." She nodded toward the pile of cookies. "About six inches was his tipping point."

Jillian released the built-up anxiety the race to get to the bakery had caused. "Paulie, what on earth are you doing here?"

The boy shoved a cookie in his mouth and spoke around his chewing. "You invited me, remember?"

"Do your parents—" Jillian stopped, remembering what Jeremiah had told her about the boy losing his father. "Does your mother know where you are?"

The boy shrugged. "She works late. Won't be home until the morning."

"How did you get here?"

"I caught a ride."

Red flags and warning bells went off in Jillian's head. "Please, Paulie, please tell me you did not hitchhike here."

"Naw, I had a friend going this way, and I asked them to drop me off on the interstate."

"You walked here from the highway?"

"I didn't walk." Paulie jutted his chin toward the door behind Jillian. A quick glance showed his skateboard leaned against the wall.

"Oh, that's so much better," Jillian said wryly. She reached for her cell phone in her back pocket. "What's your mother's number at work?"

"Aw, come on, she doesn't need to know about this. I'll be back before she gets home."

"I don't care. You're not staying here another second without her knowing you're here. Bertie, take the cookies away."

Bertie clearly wanted to protest, but she did as Jillian said and reached for the plate.

"Fine." The boy grumbled out the number to his mother's work as he pulled the plate back from Bertie's grasp. "But she's not going to like this. Her boss is really mean to her, and you calling will only get her in more trouble."

Jillian's thumb hovered over the call button. She didn't want to get the woman in trouble, maybe even risk her job. As a single parent, Paulie's mom surely struggled to provide since her husband passed away.

"Okay, I won't call. But I'm taking you to her right now."

"Aw, come on, I just got here. I like this town. It's nice." He bit a cookie. "The food's good."

Jillian wagged her finger at the boy. "Don't throw compliments at me. You're in trouble, mister. Grab your skateboard. We're leaving now."

Paulie looked longingly at the plate of cookies and frowned.

"Not to worry, Paulie," Bertie retrieved a bakery box, then returned to Paulie's table and poured the plate of cookies in the box and closed the lid. "You're good to go."

Paulie smiled up at Jillian's grandmother. "I like you too. Could you maybe throw in one or two of those cake pops I saw in the case?"

Bertie chortled. "You saw those, did you?" She picked up the box and took it behind the display case, where she grabbed two cake pops and added them to the cookies. She brought the box around to the waiting boy and leaned down to talk to him. "It's been lovely getting to know you, Paulie. You come back, ya hear? Just make sure next time you have permission from your mama."

"Yes, ma'am," he said.

"Now don't eat all those at once," Bertie warned. "Your belly won't be too pleased."

Jillian huffed. "Did he hypnotize you while I was out?"

"Nonsense. He was quite the gentleman once we got some

food into him." Bertie walked to the door to open it for them. In a conspiratorial whisper, Bertie said, "Now do come back as soon as you can, Jillian. I want to hear about your trip to Avondale."

Jillian nodded solemnly. "I wish I could say I had learned a lot today, but the only thing I found out was that Flannery Garland is engaged. Again."

"Who on earth would she marry so soon after the death of Sterling Macon? I mean Bo Tyler."

"That's easy," Paulie chimed in, not even hiding the fact that he was listening in on their quiet conversation. "It's what I came to tell you, Jillian. I overheard Travis and Ruben talking in the back lot of the bar. Flannery Garland is marrying Devon Greer. I was hoping the information would help J.D. come home. I came as soon as I heard."

Jillian frowned and tried to be stern. "You still shouldn't have made the trip without your mom knowing, but I would be lying if I said it didn't help. Now, I need to locate this Devon Greer and find out who he is."

"You're taking me to him right now," Paulie said.

Jillian did a double take. "Come again?"

"My mom cleans the offices of Fugue Labs every night. Devon Greer is the CEO. If you're taking me to my mom, then you might see him when we get there."

Jillian reached for the boy's cheeks and looked into his widening eyes. "Paulie, I have never been so conflicted. Part of me wants to yell at you. The other part of me wants to kiss you."

Paulie's face scrunched up. "Yuck!"

Bertie laughed. "I don't think he likes either of those options."

Jillian beamed down at the boy and pulled him in for a tight hug. "He should have thought of that before he showed up on my doorstep with all the answers."

Fugue Labs loomed high up on a hill when Jillian came around a bend in the narrow country road. The formidable gray concrete building's intimidating presence did little to loosen the knots in her stomach.

"It's like an old Frankenstein movie," she said, eyeing the car's digital map. "The way the road has only one destination with one way in and one way out. Your mom comes here every night?" she asked Paulie.

"Yup."

"Alone?"

"Usually. Sometimes someone is working late, but since the layoffs, not so much. Sometimes her boss is here though. She swears he shows up just to stand over her and make her feel dumb, like she can't do her job without him there. She's just cleaning the place after everyone's gone home. It's not like she's working in the lab or handling the money."

Jillian bit her tongue before saying something mean about a man she'd never met. But the cut on Earle's face had told her that Devon Greer wasn't exactly a teddy bear.

"What do they do here?"

Paulie shrugged. "My mom says it's some sort of scientific research on medicine and stuff."

Maybe the Frankenstein reference wasn't so far off the mark, she thought.

Jillian turned into a side parking lot. Two cars sat in the vast space, giving it an utterly desolate appearance. One was an old tan Nissan, the other a black Porsche.

The sign posted in front of the Porsche said *Reserved for Mr. Greer.*

Paulie pointed at the car. "It looks like he's here."

"Will he be angry if I drop you off here?"

"Probably, but my mom has brought me to work before, like when I was younger and the babysitter canceled. Now, I don't have to come because I'm older and can take care of myself. I don't need a babysitter anymore."

Jillian frowned. Considering he'd managed to catch a ride two counties over without anyone knowing, she thought Paulie was still too young to be on his own. He at least needed someone who would check in on him and be a good role model. "Are you sure about that?" she asked him. "You did just skip town without permission to come visit me."

"That's different. I came to help J.D."

Jillian wondered just how much Jeremiah Davis meant to Paulie. "Do you live near him?"

"Yeah, we're in the same trailer park. He's teaching me to play piano."

Jillian smiled at the news. "Did your mom ask him to teach you?"

"No. She actually got mad because she thinks I take up too much of his time and we can't pay him. But J.D. says he has all the time in the world for me at no charge. So she's wrong about that. I confirmed it." Paulie nodded matter-of-factly.

Jillian parked beside the Porsche and got out, Paulie following suit. She peered into the fancy car's dark windows, but a quick scan revealed nothing but a few gum wrappers in the cup holder.

"Um, Jillian do you really have to tell my mom I left town?"

"Yup. Sorry, kiddo, but your mom should know."

Paulie's shoulders slumped as he trudged to the main doors.

Jillian couldn't help grinning at his back. "What will your mom do, you think?"

Paulie hugged his skateboard and cookies close. "I've never done this, so I don't know." When they reached the door, he pushed the intercom button. "Usually there's a security guard, but I don't think anyone's here tonight."

"Is that strange?"

"I think so." He pushed the button again.

Twice in one day, Jillian came upon a place where the staff had disappeared. And both times, Devon Greer had been present.

A shadowy figure appeared behind the security glass and, just as the door opened, Paulie muttered, "That's Mr. Greer."

Devon Greer was tall and blond, with a square jaw that ticked as he chomped a piece of gum between his white teeth. "Can I help you?" He studied Jillian, then dropped his piercing, unamused gaze to Paulie.

"I'm sorry to bother you after hours, but this is Paulie. Your housekeeper is his mom. I need to bring him to her."

"Hello, Mr. Greer," Paulie squeaked as he shuffled his feet.

Devon's eyes squinted tight and his jaw paused as he seemingly debated whether or not to let them in. He scrutinized them both for so long that Jillian thought for sure he would close the door on them.

"Oh, I remember you," Devon finally said to Paulie. "Sure, come on in. Your mom is on the second floor tonight."

"She works alone?" Jillian asked casually. "Seems like a big place to handle by herself."

"The rest of the crew will be arriving soon. Mia gets extra hours by coming in earlier in the evening." Devon gave Jillian a small smile over Paulie's head. The silent message between them clearly stated that his actions were meant to help the small family out. He even winked conspiratorially as though Jillian were in on it too.

Jillian offered a nod in understanding, but she really didn't understand at all. Either Devon Greer was kindhearted and generous, or he was a liar. Jillian felt inclined to believe Devon was pretending to be something he wasn't with her right now. She figured she would go along with his act for the time being. If he really was a killer, she wasn't exactly in a safe position to call him out on it.

As their footsteps echoed in the dimly lit halls of Fugue Labs, the name Flannery Garland stalled on Jillian's tongue. But how to broach the topic? "I'm Jillian Green, by the way, from Moss Hollow. Have you ever heard of the town?" Jillian hoped the questions would lead in the right direction.

"I certainly have. Pretty little place. I actually have business dealings with some people there."

Business dealings, he says. Like murder and marriage? Those kinds of business dealings?

"In fact, I was just there this morning," Devon offered, cutting into Jillian's inquisitive thoughts.

I know you were. She wanted to say it aloud and stop beating around the bush. Instead, she asked nonchalantly, "What brought you to Moss Hollow?"

Devon hit the button to the elevator. "Well, to be honest, it wasn't actually a business visit. I asked my girl to marry me today. She's from there, and I went to ask her father for her hand."

Jillian's stomach knotted up in a twist. Didn't he mean batter the father into submission?

"Oh, that's wonderful!" She feigned excitement. "Congratulations. How exciting." Jillian hoped her real feelings stayed hidden, but her acting skills never were that great.

The metal doors opened, and Devon accompanied them onto the elevator. The doors closed them inside, and Jillian could only hope she'd made a wise decision in coming to Fugue Labs. Close proximity made for an uncomfortable silence on the way up to the second floor. When the doors opened, Jillian practically pushed Paulie out so they could escape the cramped quarters.

A vacuum cleaner could be heard down a long hall, and Paulie took off to find his mother. Jillian started to follow close behind, but Devon took a slower pace, and she felt obligated to reduce her speed to match.

"Her name is Flannery Garland," Devon said quietly. Jillian glanced out the corner of her eye to see him watching her intently. "But I guess you already knew that, didn't you?"

Her feet faltered and she came to a stop. When she turned to look at him straight on, she saw that the tick had returned to his jaw, but it didn't appear to be from chewing gum now.

Down the hall, the vacuum shut down, and Paulie and his mother appeared from within an office. "Mr. Greer, I apologize for my son's intrusion."

Devon beamed with a white-toothed smile. "Nonsense, Mia. Why don't you get the boy home and take the rest of the night off. The rest of the crew can handle things."

Paulie gazed up at his mother with worry etched on his little face. His mother's face drained of color, and Jillian wondered at the reason.

Devon Greer's act of kindness seemed to make everyone uneasy, especially when he had given off a distinctly sinister vibe minutes before. Why the abrupt change? Or had Jillian simply imagined the ominous note in his voice? It came and went so fast, she couldn't be sure.

"Mr. Greer, I will come in extra early tomorrow," Mia rushed to say as she and Paulie entered the elevator. Jillian followed mother and son, glad to see Devon stay behind on the second floor. Jillian had had enough of the place and its CEO.

As soon as the doors closed, Jillian introduced herself to Mia and told her how she came to bring Paulie to her, but the tiny woman only offered a vague nod of acknowledgment that she even heard Jillian speak. She had yet to replenish her healthy color.

"Mia, you seem tense. Can I help?" Jillian asked.

"I can't lose this job," Mia replied in a whisper.

"Is Mr. Greer that hard of a boss?"

Mia shook her head. "Not always. Sometimes Mr. Greer is kind, like just now. It's his boss who never is. I wouldn't be the least bit surprised if I get fired when they find out I left early."

"I thought Devon Greer was the CEO."

"He is, but the board of directors can fire people too. Even Mr. Greer, from what I hear. It's the people we don't see who scare me."

You and me both.

The elevator opened. The night sky was growing inky beyond the entrance doors, and Jillian made a beeline for freedom from this strange place.

"I hope you don't lose your job, Mia, but if you don't mind me saying, you should consider other options anyway. This place has a heavy cloud over it. It feels like a prison to me."

Mia frowned. "Paulie, go sit in the car," she instructed her son.

"Aww, Mama, do I have to?"

"Yes. Now shoo."

"Bye, Jillian. Tell J.D. I said hi."

"I will, Paulie. Come see me again sometime—with your mom."

"Okay." He slumped off to the car.

When the Nissan's passenger door slammed shut, Mia turned to Jillian. "Will Jeremiah be found guilty?"

"You don't waste time," Jillian said, a little astonished at the previously timid woman's boldness. "I'm hoping it doesn't get that far. I'm trying to help prove he's innocent."

Mia glanced past Jillian's shoulder to study the tall, ominous building behind her. "People like Jeremiah and me don't catch breaks." Mia barked out a short, bitter laugh. "We even get in trouble for helping little old ladies."

"You mean like the widow Jeremiah helped?"

"I'm glad he told you. It was a brave move going up against the faceless people at the top."

"What do you mean? He ratted out Bo Tyler. I wouldn't consider him a man at the top."

Mia's eyes flickered. "Bo Tyler is dead, Miss Green. And Jeremiah didn't kill him. That should tell you something." Mia started walking away. "Thank you for bringing Paulie home," she called over her shoulder. "That was mighty kind of you."

Jillian wasn't ready to end the conversation, but she knew she couldn't push Mia. The single mom had another person to consider before she could just go blabbing about the people she feared so much, and Jillian would respect that.

She made her way to her own vehicle that now sat all alone in the empty parking lot.

What happened to the Porsche? The car that had been beside hers was gone. *But how?*

She glanced up at the building as Mia's car disappeared down the winding road, leaving Jillian alone in this strange and desolate place. With her heart pounding heavily in her chest, she couldn't get out of there fast enough herself.

She floored the gas pedal to get as far away from the building as fast as she could. About two miles out, Jillian slowed down and pulled over. She took out her phone and entered a few words into the search engine: *Fugue Labs Board of Directors.*

Up popped the company's About Us page with five names, two of which jumped out at Jillian instantly.

Lucinda Atwood and Earle Garland. And according to the list, Lucinda sat as president.

Was Lucinda the one in charge of Fugue Labs, striking fear into hearts as the fierce leader capable of firing at will? Had Jeremiah reached out to the widow to inform her she was being swindled by Bo Tyler, only to be alerting the fox herself?

But what if Earle Garland was the big, mean boss? Perhaps the cut on his face was more about demands he placed on Devon Greer rather than having anything to do with Flannery. But why would Devon strike Earle if he wanted his daughter's hand in marriage?

Jillian dropped her head back on the seat in frustrated confusion. Whatever was going on here, she was missing the link to make sense of it all. Did she dare make another trip to Avondale to try to talk to Flannery?

She shivered at the thought. The place gave her the willies. She pulled her car back out onto the road and made a U-turn to get back on the highway. But before she could complete her turn, her Prius jolted off to the right so hard, her small compact car spun completely around and came to a halt facing the other direction.

The impact was so fast and out of left field, it took Jillian a moment to process what had happened.

Someone had struck her.

A look in her rearview mirror caught the red taillights of a sports car. It was too dark to catch the color, but Jillian was willing to bet Possum's stash of bacon it belonged to Flannery Garland.

But what if it didn't?

She tried to put the car into gear to go after the assailant, but her hands shook so bad it was hard to grip the wheel. She didn't dare drive anywhere for a while. Besides, what did she plan to do if she caught up to her attacker?

One thing was clear: They meant business.

16

"Care to explain the scratch and dent in the Prius?" Bertie asked Jillian the next morning in the Belle Haven kitchen. The sky was starting to lighten, but a few sparkling stars hung on.

"Aren't you going to ask if I'm all right first?" Jillian took a bite of banana and washed it down with coffee. She had slept late and was now feeling rushed to get to the bakery on time. "And why aren't you at the bakery yet? We don't both need to be late."

"I called Lenora to tell her to start without us. I thought we needed to chat first."

"Chat?" Jillian drained the cup and stood up to deposit it in the sink. "Don't you mean you lecture and I listen?" At Bertie's raised eyebrows, Jillian knew she'd gone too far with her grandmother. She let out a deep sigh and leaned against the counter. "I'm sorry, Bertie. It's been a rough couple of days. Can we start again?"

"I think we'd better, and without the sass this time," Bertie replied sternly. "The car can be fixed, but it's what caused the damage to it that I'm worried about. Tell me what's going on."

"If only I knew, Bertie." Jillian recounted everything that had happened the previous evening after she and Paulie had left the bakery: Driving him to Fugue Labs, meeting Devon Greer, learning about the fear that the company cultivated in its workers. Then she told her about being hit on the way home. "It was some sort of sports car that hit me. I know Flannery drives a little red coupe, so it could easily have been her."

"Or it could have easily been any other sports car driver out for a good time on the country roads last night." Bertie fixed her gaze on Jillian. "What is it about Flannery that has you in a bother?

141

Just because the woman can't decide on a husband doesn't make her a murderer."

Jillian gaped at Bertie.

"What did I say?" Bertie asked. "You look as lost as last year's Easter egg."

"That's it, Bertie. The missing link to put this whole mess back together. Why is Flannery in a rush to find a husband?"

"Shouldn't the question be why aren't you in more of a rush?"

Jillian wasn't about to let Bertie drag her into another conversation about Hunter's intentions. "I'm going to let that slide since, thanks to you, I have a destination again."

"And where's that, dear?"

"The mother of the bride will know everything there is to know."

Bertie's expression grew puzzled. "Flannery's mother died years ago. It was tragic. The woman was eccentric and did some strange things, but it was still so sad for Flannery and her father to lose her."

"I know Blanche Garland is dead. I wasn't talking about her. I was talking about the woman who fills the role for Flannery now. Considering what I found out last night at Fugue Labs and her connection to Flannery, it seems everything comes back to Lucinda Atwood."

With so many roads leading to Lucinda, Jillian followed the one that would take her directly to Jardin d'Amandes once again. An afternoon lull gave her the opportunity to drive over to the enormous mansion. As she pulled onto the magnolia-lined street that led to the house, her cell phone rang. Seeing that it was Laura Lee calling, Jillian pulled over quickly to answer.

"Hi, Laura Lee," she said in greeting. "What's up?"

"Not that I should be encouraging you, but I thought you'd be interested to hear what came of a background search into Bo Tyler."

"I'm all ears."

"It turns out that he was employed at Fugue Labs for a six-month period earlier this year. And get this—some idiot assigned him to the accounting department."

"Brilliant. I mean your discovery, not the fact that someone assigned a career criminal to handle the money."

"It screams of a setup to me."

"Is that your professional opinion?"

Laura Lee laughed. "Something like that."

"So who hired Bo? Was it Lucinda Atwood?"

"That I can't find out without a court order. I'll get on it, but it could take some time."

"I just pulled up to Lucinda's house. I'll see if she knows what happened." *After I ask her a few other things—if I get the chance.*

"I'd tell you to stay out of it, but I know it won't do any good. Be safe, Jillian," Laura Lee said before she disconnected the call.

Jillian stared at the house looming beyond the iron gate and collected her thoughts. Jeremiah had saved Lucinda from Bo Tyler's schemes to embezzle money out of Fugue Labs. She could have had Bo killed in retribution, but justice could have been served a lot cleaner than a knife in the back.

Lucinda could have also had Bo Tyler killed to keep him silent about who hired him, especially if she was the one to set him up to get her money out of Fugue Labs. Perhaps she was just cleaning up after her own dirty deeds.

Or maybe she had him killed just to get him out of Flannery's life. Lucinda knew Bo Tyler was a thief and wouldn't want Flannery being used. And perhaps, as Devon Greer's boss, she believed him to be a more suitable match for her surrogate daughter. Did Lucinda prefer Devon for Flannery? Is that why the proposal had come so quickly after Bo's death?

Jillian opened her car door and stepped out. It was time to get to the bottom of the whole situation. Around the front of her Prius, she quickly glanced at the passenger side and frowned at the scratches and dents caused by last night's hit-and-run. With a sigh, she realized she'd need to call her insurance company as soon as possible. *What a pain*, she thought, then caught herself. She was lucky to be unharmed. If the driver had really wanted to hurt her, it would have been only too easy. She was grateful that whoever it was had clearly only wanted to scare her.

The gate swung open smoothly, and the walk up to the front door was uneventful. Standing on the porch, Jillian peered through the thin, etched window on the side of the door. All seemed at peace in the stoic home.

She rapped the knocker and waited for the door to open, hoping it wouldn't be slammed shut on her again. Jillian braced a foot to be at the ready to stop Lucinda from closing her out.

The door swung wide open to reveal the older woman. Instead of saying a word, she stepped aside so Jillian could pass through. Jillian stood still, a bit stunned by such a different experience from last time. It felt like Lucinda had been expecting her.

"Aren't you coming in, Miss Green?" Lucinda asked in an annoyed voice.

Jillian stepped over the threshold warily. "Were you expecting me?"

"I figured you would be back eventually." The woman turned her back on Jillian and made her way through the grand hall to a side parlor.

Jillian took that as an indication that she was supposed to follow. She shut the door quickly and caught up to Lucinda as she passed by the grand piano Jeremiah had played the night of the fund-raiser. Apparently the instrument had been wheeled back into this room after his performance in the hall. The old woman reverently touched the surface and traced its glossy black finish. She stopped and let her fingers linger a moment before lifting them away and curling them into her frail palm.

"When I heard Jeremiah playing this piano the night of the fund-raiser, I wept." Lucinda glanced at Jillian, but her gaze seemed to go through her, as if she were seeing another place, another time. "It's why I remained upstairs for so long that night. If Earle hadn't come to get me, I just might have stayed there for the whole evening." She looked back at the spot where Jeremiah had sat at the keys. "He was the first person to play this instrument since my husband passed away. I wasn't prepared for the sound of the first notes lifting to my bedroom above." Her face took on a dreamy expression. "And then I began to hum along, just like in the old days. Alan, my husband, would play and I would sing along."

"You both had a love for music, then." Jillian examined the room for evidence of Lucinda's dead husband. A single framed photograph sat above the fireplace, but it was all the way over on the other side of the long room and too far away to tell if it was of the late Alan Atwood.

"I understand you haven't been in Moss Hollow for very long," Lucinda said abruptly. "Is that correct?"

"I grew up here, but I left for California more than twenty years ago. It's only recently that I've returned to help my grandmother with the bakery. Why do you ask?"

"I was trying to figure out if you knew how my Alan died."

Jillian bit the inside of her cheek to keep from asking, not wanting to be so crass—especially when Lucinda had just admitted to missing his piano playing. But why had Lucinda brought up her husband's death? Had it been under mysterious conditions?

Could Lucinda herself have been suspected? "No," she replied, trying to keep her voice even, "I don't know. I think it happened before I got back. What a horrible loss for you. My grandmother was devastated when my grandfather passed."

"It was horrible," Lucinda agreed as she approached an ornate brocade-covered sofa that stood against the wall. She bowed her head and reached for the end table's drawer. It slid open without a sound, and she reached into it. "He passed so suddenly. One day all was well, and the next he was gone. I didn't even have time to say goodbye." Her voice cracked.

Jillian glued her gaze to Lucinda's hidden hand, then shifted her feet closer to the exit in case she needed to make a run for it. Images of sharp letter openers flashed in her mind. She could dodge a knife, but not a gun. And even little old Lucinda could pull a trigger.

"He was a good man, a much better person than I. I never understood what he saw in me." Lucinda sniffled and pulled her hand out from the drawer. "His heart just didn't hold out."

Jillian tensed, ready to spring.

A handkerchief flashed white as Lucinda shook it open with a flourish.

Jillian let out a sigh of relief and slumped to the piano bench.

"Are you ill, dear?" Lucinda asked. She pressed the cloth to her glistening eyes.

"I'm fine, really," Jillian said, swallowing a relieved giggle. "Forgive me. My nerves have been stretched tight lately. How did Mr. Atwood pass?"

"A massive heart attack."

"I'm sorry, Mrs. Atwood. Really. That must have been so hard for you."

"Much harder because he left me the business to run. I couldn't grieve him properly because I had to jump right into running the business. I couldn't let his life's work fail."

"Fugue Labs?" Jillian perked up. *Now we're talking.* "I know you sit on the board as president. Was that not by choice?"

"It was my husband's idea to make sure no one came in and changed his vision for the company. He worked hard to make it a success in a sea of other pharmaceutical companies."

"How long will you have to continue?"

Lucinda shrugged. "Until either I am six feet under, or the place goes under." Her smile undermined the weight of that statement.

It would appear Fugue Labs is a prison to many.

"Did you hire Bo Tyler to do the latter? Or was that someone else?" Time was ticking, and Jillian was done with the small talk.

Lucinda's lips twitched. "I hired Bo Tyler, yes. But not to steal from my company. I hired him as a favor to someone who wanted to give him a second chance in life. Beech Brook fell on hard times about ten years ago. My husband had hopes of reviving the town by bringing Fugue Labs there, but then things took a turn for the worst. Alan would be so distraught to see what has become of the town and his company. Then again, if he were here, I'm sure none of it would have happened." She sighed deeply, then shook her head briskly as if forcing herself to stop thinking about it. "But enough of that place. I know why you're really here, Jillian, but I have to tell you, I really think you need to go back to your home and bakery and let the police handle this murder investigation."

Another person with that advice? Or the same one? Jillian straightened in her seat. "I won't stop until the correct person is behind bars."

Lucinda sighed and then stuffed the handkerchief into the pocket of her pearl-gray suit coat. "Flannery did not kill Bo."

"Did I say she did?"

Lucinda grew flustered. "Fine. I won't lie." She placed her hand at her throat. "The Garland family is everything to me. I don't know where I would be today without Earle and Flannery. Our families go way back. Alan and Earle were the best of friends. The Garlands have been my only family since Alan passed. I don't know what I would do without them, and I have to ask you to stop following them. You're looking in the wrong place. Believe me when I tell you they are innocent in all this."

"How can you be so sure?"

"I can't tell you how I know. I just do."

"Why are you asking me to stop? It feels like you're covering for them."

"I would do anything for them."

"Anything?"

Lucinda's gaze darkened and locked on Jillian. Her voice deepened as she said evenly, "Anything."

Slowly, Jillian stood from the piano bench. The room fell into a heavy silence as she felt her chest tighten. Lucinda's implication that she would kill for the Garlands still didn't sit right. How could such a frail woman sink a knife into a strong, healthy man who stood at least a foot taller than her? She couldn't have done it without help, but who else would kill for the Garlands?

"Lucinda, I hope you don't really mean *anything*."

"Oh, I do. You don't understand. When I lost my Alan, there were people who tried to take advantage of me. It was the Garlands who came to my aid."

"No, it was Jeremiah Davis who told you Bo Tyler was swindling you. And now he's in jail. And it was you who brought him to Moss Hollow."

Lucinda frowned. "His incarceration is an unfortunate side effect, but there's really nothing I can do for him."

"But he put himself on the line for you."

"Well, he shouldn't have." Lucinda wrung her hands, agitation coming through.

"You're willing for Jeremiah to go to prison because the Garlands asked you to kill Bo Tyler."

"They did no such thing." Lucinda shot up out of her seat faster than Jillian would have thought her capable. "Bite your tongue. They are good people."

"So is Jeremiah Davis. In addition to helping you, did you know he mentors a young boy who lost his father a few years ago to cancer?"

"He's a thief."

"He's a product of his circumstances and has made mistakes. I'm not saying he shouldn't pay for his crimes, but *only* his crimes. So, why don't you tell me who you had kill Bo? Because we both know it wasn't Jeremiah."

Lucinda dropped back down to the brocade settee, her hands clutched so tightly together that her thin skin was discolored. Her breathing picked up to a rapid pace that concerned Jillian. The loose skin of her throat convulsed and shook when she swallowed hard.

Wondering if she could appeal to Lucinda's apparent fixation on "good people," Jillian tried another tactic. "I've met the single mother Jeremiah helps when needed. He's a good man. He helped you when he'd never even met you."

"I repaid my debt to him by hiring him for the fund-raiser. I owe him nothing else. I never told him to steal anything. He did that on his own."

"Wait, so are you saying you didn't set him up at all? That he only became a suspect because of the wallet found in his car?"

"I was trying to give him a chance, Miss Green. It saddened me to see him taken away by the police. I should have never brought him to Moss Hollow in the first place. He didn't need to get involved in this at all."

"Your plan to murder Bo Tyler, you mean?"

Lucinda dropped her gaze to her clenched hands in her lap. She couldn't look Jillian in the eyes.

"Lucinda, did you kill Bo Tyler or arrange to have him killed?"

The woman stood up abruptly. "I need to ask you to leave. This is all Jeremiah's fault. He got involved by being the scum and thief he is. He doesn't belong in society. He belongs behind bars."

Lucinda walked to the foyer, her outstretched hand leading the way to the front door. Despite her abrupt change of attitude, she still exuded hospitality. Her chin was lifted with poise, her stance that of a debutante.

"I won't let an innocent man go to jail," Jillian stated.

"He's not innocent. He stole Mr. Porter's wallet. You were there. You saw."

"What if he didn't steal anything? What if the person who really did kill Bo Tyler set the whole scene up to make sure it was Jeremiah Davis who paid the price?"

"That's ridiculous. No one knew anything about Jeremiah Davis or his past, or even where he was from."

"Bo Tyler knew. Are you sure no one else did? You must have discussed who the talent would be with the arts commission."

"I am well respected by all. I don't need approval, nor do I need to share the details of where the talent I hire comes from. They trust my judgment."

"Even over at Fugue Labs? Do you run that place too? Did you direct Devon Greer to hire and fire the workers like you hired Jeremiah?"

"How do you know Devon Greer?"

"I met him the other day. I hear he's marrying Flannery."

"What?" Lucinda's eyes grew agitated. Apparently, the upcoming nuptials were a surprise to her. "I have to go. I mean you need to go." She reached for the door, but a shout from the stairs froze both of them where they stood.

"Stop right there, both of you! No one's going anywhere."

Jillian and Lucinda whipped around to see Flannery Garland walking down the curved staircase. Despite her pink heels, she took every step with perfect, practiced grace. However, Jillian wasn't worried about the pageant queen falling—she was too distracted by the black gun in Flannery's sure and steady hand.

"Sweetheart," Lucinda said, putting her hand to her rapidly rising and falling chest. "You don't have to do this. I will protect you. Please, put the gun away and go back upstairs. You will not go to jail. I promise. I will never let that happen, even if it means I go."

Jillian tore her gaze from the gun to Lucinda and back to Flannery. Had Lucinda only been protecting her friend's daughter? When she had said she would do anything for her, did she mean even go to jail for a murder the pageant beauty committed?

Then something else occurred to Jillian: if Flannery had murdered her own fiancé, she would probably have no trouble doing the same to a mere baker.

The brocade sofa was now Jillian's witness stand, and Flannery served as her judge, jury, and executioner all rolled into one. The way she waved the gun around made Jillian flinch as the young woman paced back and forth in the parlor.

Lucinda wrung her hands once again on the sofa's other end. "Dear girl, I beg you to put that horrid thing down. It's not becoming of a lady."

"I have spent my whole life being a *lady*," Flannery cried and turned to show real tears streaming down her face. The tense week had apparently left its mark on her. Her hair was knotted in the back, and her makeup streaked her cheeks. "Everyone is always telling me what to do, where to go, what to wear. Even my dead mother is pulling my strings!" The gun waved again.

Jillian crouched out of its line of fire.

Flannery saw her duck and aimed the gun straight at her. "I am done following orders. Now you're going to follow mine."

Jillian searched Flannery's face for signs of delusion, but she only saw anguish—and that gun. "I'm sorry, Flannery." Jillian felt compelled to offer comfort, but what could she say? So, she told her what she herself might want to hear in this tense situation. "You're not alone. Lucinda wants to help you, and so do I."

"Neither of you can help me now."

"Because of your engagement to Devon Greer?" Jillian asked. "Are you being forced into that too?"

Flannery stilled. The gun slowly dropped to her side. Pain that seemed too deep for tears spread over her face, a melancholy that told Jillian that Flannery had lost every ounce of hope. She walked to the piano and put the gun on top. The barrel was still directed toward the settee, but Jillian thought she was close to getting Flannery to relinquish it. What had been dire circumstances a moment ago now seemed almost hopeful.

"I thought I'd have the last laugh," Flannery said in a subdued voice. "I should have known I couldn't." She faced Jillian, but didn't focus on her. "My mother left me a trust fund when she died. But, you see, in order for me to access the money, I have to be married by my twenty-sixth birthday. And it has to be to a man my father approves of." She slumped down on the piano bench.

The archaic absurdity of the situation caused Jillian to cringe. "Oh, how horrible, Flannery. My grandmother had mentioned your mom was eccentric, but that's beyond my imaginings. When is your twenty-sixth birthday?"

Flannery let out a short wail and dropped her head into the palm of her hand. As she did, her elbows hit the piano keys, and they let out a disjointed cacophony.

Lucinda quietly answered for Flannery. "The end of the month."

"That's less than two weeks. What happens if she's not married?"

"The money goes to charity." Lucinda's voice sounded steady, but Jillian wondered how much of it was an act.

Jillian leaned closer to the older woman and whispered, "Is it a lot of money?"

Lucinda narrowed her eyes in disdain. "Really, Miss Green, could you be more crass? Don't you know there are topics of discussion that are taboo, money being one of them?"

"Sorry." Jillian felt as though she had been sent to the principal's office. "I was only asking because I wanted to know if the amount was enough to make someone kill."

Flannery's head shot up. "Jeremiah Davis would never get a penny of my money."

"Jeremiah Davis didn't kill anyone," Jillian said sharply. Didn't these women see how Jeremiah had no reason to kill Bo Tyler? They were grasping at straws. "Why do you both want Jeremiah Davis to be convicted of murder?"

Flannery jumped to her feet. "Because he hated Sterling enough to kill him and should be punished." She wielded her gun again.

This time Jillian held firm. "His name is Bo Tyler, and you know it. Quit the hysterics and be honest. You agreed to marry Bo Tyler to gain access to your own money." Jillian stood to meet Flannery eye to eye. "The Ivy League schools, the preppy wardrobe . . . *you* made it all up. You fabricated Sterling Macon so Daddy would approve, and you would get your money. Isn't that right, Flannery?"

Lucinda frowned, tears misting her eyes. She sniffed loudly. "This is so appalling. I should have seen this coming. I should have known it could only end in disaster."

Flannery gawked at Lucinda. "You've known the whole time? You knew what we planned?"

"Since the second you brought him here for my blessing and asked me to hire him at Fugue Labs. You didn't fool me. He needed to have a good job to prove to Earle he was a worthy choice for you to marry. The man began robbing me blind and ruining the company from the inside. I couldn't believe you were in on that, but then you announced you were marrying him. That's when I began to see he was working his magic on you. You were falling for his lies. Such a despicable man." Lucinda said the words snidely with her upper lip curled in distaste. "I don't blame you, sweetheart. I blame him and his crooked ways. He would have ruined you just as he set out to ruin me. I was trying to find a way out for you. I just hadn't quite managed it yet."

"Oh, Lucinda, I'm sorry he did that to you, but that was before Sterling became a new man. He said goodbye to Bo Tyler forever. I was helping him start over, to start a life of respectability and legitimate prosperity. Sterling wasn't the same man who scammed you. If only you hadn't brought that piano man to Moss Hollow. Why did you do it?"

"We thought it was the only way to show you Sterling Macon would never change. And we were right. As soon as he saw Jeremiah Davis, he reverted right back to his lowborn, grasping self."

"No!" Flannery raised the gun again. "He was only scared that man would ruin everything we had worked for. Daddy was beginning to accept Sterling as a future son-in-law. He had given us his approval. We were going to get married before my birthday. It was all so perfect, and I would get my money *my* way. But you—" Flannery trained the gun on Lucinda "—you just had to bring that piano player here. He killed Sterling, and he killed my chances at happiness."

Huge tears welled up in Flannery's eyes again and rolled down her sculpted cheeks, smearing the mess of mascara even more. Her sharp, thin shoulders heaved forward and she crumpled in wrenching sobs. Jillian suddenly saw where the pain was coming from. It was more than losing her fiancé.

It was being forced to marry someone she hadn't chosen.

"You wouldn't be marrying Devon Greer unless you had to," Jillian said aloud as she figured it out.

Flannery gave a loud wail. She yanked a ring from her finger and chucked it against the wall. "I hate him!"

Jillian winced as the ring pinged off the wall, bounced, and skidded to a stop. The giant princess-cut diamond with its sharp corners reflected the sun's rays brightly. It had to be at least three carats. Devon Greer had done well for himself at Fugue Labs.

"You used to love him," Lucinda said in a low voice. "The way the two of you would sing and play the piano so beautifully always reminded me of the music Alan and I made."

Flannery shook her head. "That was before he became CEO of Fugue Labs. He changed. He became sneaky and selfish, and I know there were things he wouldn't tell me. And then he started laying people off. He killed a whole town. Besides, what kind of man moves in to marry someone who just lost her fiancé?"

Jillian piped up. "One that knows he could get rich?"

Flannery's attention shot toward Jillian, as did the barrel of the gun. "Exactly."

Jillian ducked. "Would you stop pointing that thing at me?"

"It's not even loaded." Flannery's revelation was made almost nonchalantly, and she continued on, oblivious to the fact that she held a lethal weapon, loaded or not. "He doesn't love me. He loves what I come with."

"And you don't think Bo Tyler did too?" Lucinda shouted in a very unladylike burst, but she recovered her composure quickly, her hand on her chest.

"Bo changed." The words sounded as though they were tearing at Flannery's heart. Was she trying to make them believe it, or herself?

Jillian didn't particularly want to tell Flannery she was lying to herself about the man, but she had to if they were going to get past this and figure out the truth. As long as Flannery believed her boyfriend had transformed into an upstanding individual, she'd continue to believe Jeremiah was the only suspect who had a reason to take him out.

"Flannery, did Bo—I mean Sterling have an allergy to nuts?"

Flannery's blotchy face stilled. She sniffed. "No, I don't think so. Why?"

"The day before the fund-raiser, he tried to scam me, saying I sold him a cookie with nuts that he was allergic to. But he had never set foot in my bakery, I'm sure of it. That doesn't sound to me like a man who had changed."

Flannery's gaze darted away from Jillian's to the vase on the piano. She stared blankly at it in a heavy silence.

"You wanted to believe he had stepped into his fabricated life and become the good man you created, but he didn't," Jillian said. "You wanted to be the one who changed him. So much so that you denied the fact that he had duped you as easily as he had duped Lucinda."

"He loved me. I know he did. He said he'd never loved anyone before because no one had ever loved him."

Jillian sighed. "Those might be the truest words he'd ever spoken. Maybe he was trying to tell you he could never love you either."

Flannery's lips trembled and she glanced down at the gun, staring at it as though it had just appeared there. She winced and put it on the piano.

Jillian made her way closer to the piano. "You tried, Flannery. No one would ever fault you for trying to show a broken man love. And maybe he died knowing he was loved for the first time in his life."

Tears spilled from Flannery's eyes. "I'll never know now, because that despicable piano man killed him so viciously."

"Jeremiah didn't kill anyone." Jillian wondered if she could grab the gun and make sure it wasn't loaded, but she didn't want to startle Flannery by making a sudden movement. She didn't want to find out the hard way if Flannery was wrong about the gun not being loaded.

"Of course he did. He'd known Sterling from the past. They hated each other. They both came from a life of crime. He was jealous of Sterling's fresh start. It makes perfect sense that he would kill him to stop him from having a legitimate life."

"Someone thought that Jeremiah was worthy of a second chance too," Jillian said. "It's why he was hired to come to Moss Hollow."

Flannery fixed her sights on Lucinda. "You hired him."

Lucinda held up her hands and shrugged. "I hired him because he helped me save my finances. That's all. I wanted to repay him for his deed."

"You wanted to get rid of Sterling, and this was your way of doing it. Did you hire that piano player to kill Sterling?"

Lucinda recoiled as though she'd been slapped. "Don't be ridiculous, child."

"But you knew bringing him here would make Sterling run."

Lucinda looked away, her hands wringing again.

"How could you do that to me?" Flannery headed for the front door, gun in hand and Lucinda and Jillian on her heels.

"How could I?" Lucinda called. "You're like a daughter to me. I couldn't stand by and let that . . . that wicked man hurt you."

Flannery stopped at the front door, her hand on the knob. Slowly, she turned and squinted at the older woman. "Before, you said 'we.'"

"Pardon me?"

Flannery jammed her finger at Lucinda. "You said, '*We* thought it was the only way to show you Sterling Macon would never change.' Who else was in on your little scheme to break my heart and ruin my life?"

Lucinda reached toward Flannery, eyes pleading. "Please try to understand."

"Just answer the question."

"Devon loves you, Flannery," Lucinda said, her voice full of emotion. "He never stopped."

Anger bleached Flannery's face white, except for two unbecoming red spots on her cheeks. She opened the door, but before she escaped through it, she shot a glance back at Lucinda. "You'll regret this." The beauty queen hurled the gun at the wall with a fierce growl, then bolted through the door. As the gun clattered to the floor, Flannery's car could be heard screaming around the side of the house and down the driveway at breakneck speed.

Jillian ran to the window just in time to see that the little red sports car's front headlight was broken. Flannery *had* hit her the night before. The girl must be out for revenge at having her plans thwarted.

"What will she do now?" Jillian asked.

Lucinda turned worried eyes on Jillian. "I've known Flannery for quite some time, and when she's like this, there's no telling what she might do."

Jillian sank deep into a lounge chair on Belle Haven's front porch. Birds chirped incessantly in the magnolia trees, and a glass of cold sweet tea sweated beside her in the warm evening air. She'd taken one sip from it after Cornelia brought it to her, but she'd forgotten about it as she recounted her harrowing adventure at gunpoint that day.

Bertie seemed like she could use something cool to drink too. As Jillian finished, her grandmother's anger boiled over. "I just can't wrap my head around the fact that Flannery Garland held you at gunpoint. Why would she do such a thing?"

Jillian exhaled heavily. "Honestly, that question is why I don't believe she killed anyone."

"But she held you at gunpoint," Cornelia said. "Doesn't that indicate that she had violence in mind?"

"It wasn't loaded. She only did it because she believed I was helping the man she thinks killed her fiancé. Her first fiancé. She wants Jeremiah to pay for killing Bo, but that's only because she believes he's guilty. She left Lucinda's today with doubts about that, which is good."

"Well, the sheriff's department has the gun and is looking for her. She could go to jail herself when they find her. Such a waste." Bertie shook her head disapprovingly.

Jillian agreed, but she'd felt compelled to report that Flannery had threatened her and Lucinda with a gun and that the formerly sweet-natured beauty queen had run away from Jardin d'Amandes in a distraught state . . . especially if she went after Devon Greer next. "I'm sorry about that, but it was her choice. She smashed her car into mine and held a gun on me. Lucinda too. A woman who loves her like she was her own daughter."

Cornelia harrumphed. "She must have really loved Bo. It's so sad to see such a strong woman blind to his crooked ways."

"Maybe her love did change him a bit," Jillian suggested. "I don't know why, but part of me wants that for her. To believe that love can change a person, turn them away from a life of crime."

Bertie reached over and squeezed Jillian's hand. "You have a good heart, dear. I only wish it didn't get you into so much trouble. I also wish I could have seen you stand up to Flannery and her gun."

A car turned at the end of the drive. Hunter's silver Lexus came into view, racing toward Belle Haven.

"It looks like someone just found out about the day's events," Cornelia said.

The Lexus screeched to a halt. The driver's door flew wide, and Hunter burst out of the vehicle and sprinted toward the porch without bothering to close the door behind him.

Jillian wasted no time gaining her feet. As she stood, Hunter reached her and wrapped his arms around her, then held her close for several emotional moments.

Finally, he pulled back and stared into her eyes, then dropped his forehead to hers. "I just heard what happened. I had to see you, to know you were safe."

Jillian scarcely dared to breathe. She waited for him to say, "I told you so." He had every right to, and she braced herself for his judgment. She dropped her eyes away from his, not wanting to see the criticism in his eyes.

"You are so brave," he whispered. "I've never met anyone like you."

"Is that good?" she asked, unsure if the conversation would stay in her favor.

His charming smile broke over his face, and he took her hands and squeezed them. "I wouldn't have it any other way."

"Even when I don't do as you tell me and stay out of danger?"

"When have I ever been able to tell you to do anything?"

"Doesn't keep you from trying."

"What good that does me. I just wish I could have been there."

"What, to save me?" Jillian asked.

He laughed. "No, to see you in action."

Bertie cleared her throat. "Cornelia, will you help me in the kitchen? I think I heard something crash."

"I didn't hear anything but two lovebirds," Cornelia answered.

Jillian inhaled sharply, but before she could ask what the two women were talking about, the sound of another car turning in at the end of the driveway stole the moment.

"I wonder who that is." Bertie squinted at the black limousine creeping closer and coming to a stop behind Hunter's Lexus.

The engine switched off and a chauffeur stepped out from behind the wheel. He came around to the other side and opened the rear door for all on the porch to see.

Reaching inside the vehicle, he gave his hand to Lucinda Atwood.

"What on earth is she doing here?" Cornelia approached the end of the porch. The rest of them followed her until they stood clustered in a group watching the old woman amble up the path with her driver at her arm. They stopped at the base of the porch, Lucinda's hand trembling on the man's forearm.

"Please, Miss Green," Lucinda said in a shaky voice. "Tell the police my Flannery meant no harm. Let her come home to me."

All eyes turned to Jillian, who struggled to find a quick reply. "I'm sorry, Mrs. Atwood, but she had a gun."

"It wasn't loaded. You know that."

"That doesn't matter."

"Flannery is confused and hurt. You must see how she

feels trapped."

"I see a wise, experienced woman coddling another grown woman."

Lucinda sighed. "This is all my fault. I should have never brought Jeremiah Davis to Moss Hollow. I should have believed in Flannery and let her make her own choices, supporting her instead of trying to control her. I was just so afraid she would ruin her life."

"We only ever want the best for those we love," Bertie said with a meaningful glance at Jillian, who gave her a small smile.

Lucinda continued. "That's why I'm here. To fix my mistakes and to finish what I have started. I want to help my Flannery find a second chance at a happy life."

"But how? Bo Tyler is dead, and unless she marries Devon, her money is gone too."

"I know. I can't change that. But I can make sure the real killer is behind bars . . . and I can make sure Flannery doesn't marry him before that."

Jillian blinked, trying to process the revelation that Lucinda had just dropped on them all. "Are you saying Devon Greer is Bo Tyler's killer?"

"It's quite possible. It was Devon's idea to bring Jeremiah here in the first place. He was convinced that the only way Flannery would see Bo Tyler as the criminal he was would be for one of his own to bring it out in him. And it worked. Bo lost it when he saw Jeremiah at the keys with Flannery singing. The setup was a success."

"So you knew Bo would be killed?" Jillian asked, eyes wide.

"Of course not." Lucinda placed her hand over her heart. "Devon never said anything about murder. He only planned to be there for Flannery when she learned her fiancé was not worthy of her. Devon would pick up the pieces and give her his love instead. I would be lying if I said I wouldn't have preferred a match between

Flannery and Devon. But never by means of murder."

Jillian believed Lucinda to be telling the truth. "And now you know a marriage between them could be dangerous."

"If Devon killed Bo, then yes, I have to stop it. And I have to help Flannery clear her name after today. Please, Miss Green. I've talked to Flannery. She says that if Jeremiah didn't kill Bo, then she will do whatever she must to see him freed and the real killer put behind bars."

An idea bubbled up in Jillian's mind that might bring the real killer out of his tower. But this time she wanted it on her own turf.

"I'd like to throw Flannery and Devon an engagement party right here at Belle Haven. All I need is the name of a good piano tuner."

Lucinda furrowed her brow. "That's it?"

"Well, a piano tuner and Flannery's willingness to put on a good song and dance. And I don't just mean the musical variety. It might mean she loses everything she holds dear when the truth comes out. The same goes for you. It could cost you everything."

Concern etched Lucinda's face. Saying she wanted the truth and actually sacrificing for it were two different things.

Finally, with a deep sigh of resolve, she said, "Alan would want me to know the truth. He never made a decision without making sure he had the full picture, but he was also a shrewd businessman because he was willing to risk everything for the greater good. I did everything I could to hold on to his hard work, especially for the employees of Fugue Labs. Alan had a vision for the town of Beech Brook that I'm sad to say never took off because I let others handle more of the business than I should have after Alan's passing. They took advantage of me. It's so hard to know who you can trust, Jillian. But like Alan, I'm willing to risk it all for the greater good." Lucinda gave a firm nod. "Assuming this means you'll call off the police from this whole silly gun business, you can count on Flannery, and you can count on me. When does the show start?"

Jillian beamed at Lucinda. "Because of the pressing matter of Flannery's trust fund, time is of the essence. Let's plan for Saturday night at eight o'clock."

Cornelia clapped her hands joyously. "A summer night of singing and dancing at Belle Haven. Could there be anything lovelier?"

"Please try to focus on the fact that we're trying to catch a killer, Sister," Bertie scolded.

Hunter cleared his throat. "I hate to be the bearer of bad news, but we don't have a piano player. He's in jail."

Jillian smiled and tilted her head in Hunter's direction. "I have some ideas where I can find one. Not to worry." She gave Hunter's hand a squeeze, letting him know she liked having him beside her, taking part in this.

"We have a singer and a piano, I can get you a piano tuner, and you'll find the piano man," Lucinda said. "But I just don't understand how we will free Jeremiah Davis with a party."

Slow satisfaction morphed Jillian's face into a smug smile. "We're going to call the killer's bluff."

Ken's Piano Bar was just as deserted as it had been the first time Jillian had stepped inside. She and Hunter did a quick survey through the dimly lit interior and found a shadowed man hunkered over a drink at the bar. The way he was huddled sent a clear "do not disturb" message. Jillian bypassed the man to see the same bartender from before, the slender woman with straight dark hair, standing behind the bar at the register. She wasn't jumping up to greet them either.

A slow, choppy tune from the piano broke the stifled atmosphere. Jillian expected to find Travis entertaining again, but a glance toward the piano showed Ruben at the keys instead.

Hunter reached for Jillian's hand. She expected him to drag her out of the bar, but instead of leading her to the door, he guided her to the piano.

She listened to the music, which improved as Ruben warmed up. The slow jazz melody he played was haunting, and she placed a hand on the instrument as the tune affected her. The man's eyes were hidden behind dark shades and, from the way he held his head up, Jillian realized the man who usually smoked alone in the corner booth was blind. Was that why he hadn't come out from his table the last time she was there? It was obviously why he'd refused to look at the photo of Bo. He had seemed so cagey, but maybe his blindness isolated him.

"Someone's at my piano," Ruben said. His fingers didn't even stumble over the keys as he spoke. "You're touching it. I can tell by how the music changed."

Jillian yanked her hand back, prompting a raspy cackle from the pianist. "I'm sorry, I didn't know," she said.

He laughed again, louder with his head thrown back. "I'm just pulling your leg. Welcome back, Miss Jillian. What brings you to Ken's this time?"

"Um . . ." She grew flustered at his use of her name. How did he know it was her? Maybe he wasn't totally blind.

While she tried to piece that puzzle together, Hunter asked, "Who exactly is Ken?"

Ruben played on without responding. Instead, the woman at the bar replied in her serrated voice. "I'm Ken. This is my place, and Ruben asked you a question. What brings you back here?"

Jillian swung around to face the woman who didn't seem so

excited to see her again. "You're Ken?"

"Short for Kendra. And yes, I own this place . . . for now. Tough to run a piano bar without a piano player."

"Do you play?" Jillian asked.

"Not well. I usually leave the playing to the boys. I just pour the drinks. What'll it be?"

Jillian looked to Hunter, then to Ruben. "Nothing for us. We're actually here to ask you for help."

Ken crossed her arms. "Times are too hard for me to deal with loiterers. You can order something or you can leave. Either way, I'd appreciate it if you didn't harass my musician. I don't need to lose another one."

Jillian couldn't argue with that. "All right. Could we have a couple sweet teas and maybe an order of fries?"

Ken gave a sharp nod and bustled around getting their order.

Ruben finished the song and launched into another as though no one had spoken.

Jillian faltered, not knowing how to bring up what she needed after what could only be described as a rather chilly reception.

Both Ruben and Ken seemed to forget she and Hunter were there. Getting help from these people could be harder than she thought. When Ken served the teas and fries on the bar, Hunter retrieved them and brought them back to Jillian, who was beginning to feel awkward beside the piano.

Finally she worked up the nerve to ask Ruben, "Where's the other player? The one who was here before? Travis, I believe." He had helped her—on the sly, but it had definitely helped. "Please. I don't mean any harm. I want to hire him to play at an engagement party."

"You don't say," Ruben replied. There wasn't even a hint of merriment in his voice. "Who's getting hitched?"

"Devon Greer and Flannery Garland. But I know you already

know that. Paulie told me he heard the news from you."

Ruben sat stoned-faced, and Jillian thought he might refuse to answer, but then he growled, "Why would you want to throw Devon Greer an engagement party?"

Jillian hesitated. The less people knew, the better chance Devon would show up. "It's more to support Flannery," she said as a way of sidestepping his question. "She'd like to sing for her fiancé in a public setting, but I need a piano player to accompany her. I was hoping Travis would be here."

Ken chimed in from behind. "Travis would never play for that man. It's well-known around these parts that Devon Greer is the reason Fugue Labs is in shambles. If you haven't seen the town out there, it's pretty bad. The few people of Beech Brook who still work up there need their jobs, especially since so many, like Travis, lost theirs."

Jillian took a chance. "What if the event was more for taking Devon Greer down?"

Ruben played a fast, tinkling scale across the keys. "Tell me more."

"I can't, but believe me when I say I'm just trying to make sure an innocent man doesn't go to jail for a crime he didn't commit. A crime I believe Devon Greer had more of a motive to commit."

Ruben seemed to be softening. "We heard what you did for Mia and Paulie. We appreciated it. And Jeremiah would too."

Jillian brushed Ruben's gratitude aside. "I couldn't turn the boy away."

"There have been many others who have. You're kind and smart. I like that."

"So, you think I'm onto something with Devon?"

Ruben tilted his head in thought. "It makes sense. Jeremiah definitely caused Greer some problems by alerting the authorities about Bo and his sticky fingers. Rumor had it that Greer was the one who helped Bo out, but they never proved nothing. Getting rid of both Bo and Jeremiah would leave no proof behind of his part in the scam."

"So, get rid of Jeremiah, and nobody is left to point fingers," Hunter said.

Jillian hummed in understanding. "And get rid of Bo Tyler, aka Sterling Macon, and the coast is clear for marrying Flannery Garland for more of that money he can't get enough of."

"The two of them dated pretty seriously some years back," Ken offered. "We were shocked to hear they'd broken up, but glad she didn't stand by a man who was putting employees out of work. Theft affects everyone."

"Flannery said he was a horrible man," Jillian said to Hunter. "This must be what she meant. She found out about Devon's dealings and how they affected innocent people. She wanted nothing to do with a thief. And now she's beside herself that she feels forced to marry him."

"We need to stop him before others are hurt," Hunter added. He turned to Ruben. "But we need your help finding a piano player."

Ruben raised an eyebrow from behind his shades. "That doesn't sound like the way to catch a killer."

"It will be if the killer takes the bait," Jillian said.

Ruben whistled. "Now that would be something to see."

"So you'll help us find Travis?" Jillian felt a twinge of hope.

Ken frowned. "I haven't seen Travis in a week. He said he was taking off to see a friend about a job. I'm not sure where he is, or if he'll be back. And now I've lost both my piano men." She held up a hand. "And don't look at me to help. These fingers don't tickle the ivories."

Jillian glanced at Ruben, who was already shaking his head.

"I'm not much of a player," he said.

"You have some talent. And I'm sure Flannery can make up for any mistakes."

Ruben shook his head. "I wouldn't feel right. I'm no Jeremiah or Travis."

"Well, they're not available just now, and one of them is depending on you."

Ruben sighed. "You really know how to go in for the kill. Sorry, poor choice of words."

"Say you'll do it and I'll lay off." Jillian smiled.

Ruben's fingers hit the keys and after a few trills, he transitioned into "Let the Good Times Roll."

Jillian took that as a yes.

"He's not here," Savannah said, poking her head into the Belle Haven kitchen. "What kind of fiancé doesn't show up for his own engagement party?"

Jillian picked up a plate of hors d'oeuvres and brushed past Savannah, whispering, "One who maybe got word this was a setup."

Savannah followed in step, holding a stack of napkins. "That's what I was thinking too. What are we going to do? We have police in tuxedos ready to make an arrest, thanks to Laura Lee. What if it doesn't happen?"

Jillian lifted her plate to a couple chatting by a potted fern. "Crab puff?" she asked. After each of the guests took a serving from her tray and a napkin from Savannah, the women moved along toward more partygoers mingling by the stairs. "If an arrest doesn't happen, then the officers will have a free night out. I'm not worried about them. I'm more concerned with the fact that Jeremiah will spend the rest of his life in jail."

Savannah sighed. "You're right." She grabbed the plate from Jillian. "Let the Sweetie Pies take care of this. We're all here, except for Annalise."

Jillian frowned. "Byron again?"

"When he works late, Annalise goes in with him to try to help. The bank doesn't want to hire him an assistant, so they gave her permission to help until this project is done."

"That sounds like a lot to handle."

Savannah nodded. "She never complains, but I know the long hours and Byron's grumpiness are wearing on her. Poor Annalise. And poor Jeremiah, while we're spreading pity around. At least we can help one of them. Go do what we have planned to free Jeremiah. We're here when you need us."

Jillian could have grabbed her friend and kissed her cheek, but that would lead to crab puffs staining their silky summer dresses. Unlike how out of place she'd felt at Sweet Sounds, Jillian had opted for the help to fit in with their attire tonight, rather than wear uniforms. Besides, they'd needed more people looking like guests when the party had been planned at the last minute.

Time to con the con man, she thought, and nearly chuckled. *So this is what it feels like to be on the mastermind side of a setup, or takedown, or whatever it's called.* If Jillian was going to cook up a scam, she was glad to be on the right side of the law doing it.

She stepped out onto the porch to see if any more cars were pulling up. Hunter was in place as a valet. He turned from his post and flashed his bright smile her way. She thought she would never tire of seeing his handsome face directed at her with that disarming grin. She dismissed the thought as a car turned at the end of the drive and zipped down the path.

A black Porsche. Devon had arrived.

"You're on," she called to Hunter.

Jillian rushed back inside toward the library and found Ruben standing near the piano. "Warm up those fingers," she told him.

He nodded, swept his coattails out behind him, and took a seat at the piano. He stretched his hands, then lowered his fingers to the keys. As music began to float from the instrument, Jillian was gratified to hear that Lucinda's tuner had done his job well.

Jillian entered the library and found Lucinda, Earle, and Flannery at the far end of the room, away from the night's festivities.

"Can I get you anything?" Jillian asked them as she approached.

"We are well taken care of, Ms. Green. Thank you," Earle said respectfully.

Jillian noted that the cut on Earle's right cheek had yet to heal. She forced herself not to stare at him and focused instead on Flannery. She didn't want to appear rude, but she wished she could tell Earle that Devon would get his due tonight for striking him. But confidentiality was a must if they were to succeed. She couldn't let anything compromise the plan.

"I believe your fiancé has just arrived," Jillian told Flannery in a low voice. Flannery nodded, her face pale but set. They'd decided not to tell anyone, not even Lucinda, the particular details of their plan to free Flannery from Devon's clutches as well as Jeremiah from his jail cell. To all the guests, this evening would appear as nothing more than a celebration of a future marriage.

In addition to a stunning shell-pink dress with an intricate lace overlay, Flannery wore a gracious expression. She took a deep breath as if to calm her nerves, then smoothed her gown with trembling fingers. Lucinda reached a hand out to her, and Flannery grasped it, then took her father's hand as well.

"You look beautiful, darling," Earle said.

Jillian saw that Flannery wore Devon's engagement ring again. *The thing could maim someone.*

"Thank you, Daddy. Thank you for helping me see this is for the best."

"And I promise you I will be by your side through it. He won't hurt you. I won't allow it."

"I know the time for a marriage of love has come to the end." Flannery's words sounded quite contrite and genuine. "I wish Sterling hadn't died, and I wish Mother hadn't been so manipulative with her money, even if she meant well and just wanted me to find someone who would take care of me."

Earle frowned. "I'm sure she never thought it would come to you having to marry for convenience. She loved you dearly."

"I know, and honestly, I gave up on marrying for love a long time ago. Even Sterling was for convenience. But whatever happens,

I am so blessed to have you and Lucinda standing beside me. After this wedding, Devon will be a part of our lives forever, but you two will always be my family."

"As it should be." Earle leaned over to kiss his daughter's forehead.

"When do we begin the show?" Lucinda asked.

Earle patted Lucinda's free hand. "You sound just as excited as I am to see our Flannery perform. She is so talented. It's a shame she never made it to Nashville or Hollywood. She could have been a star."

"Daddy, stop," Flannery gushed. "You have to say that. You're my father."

"I would never lie to you. You have so much promise. Now get out there and show everyone, including your future husband, who's running the show. Let him know now you're in charge."

"Oh, just you wait, Daddy. I plan to do precisely that." Flannery sent a wink Jillian's way. "Devon won't know what hit him."

Jillian trailed behind Lucinda and the Garlands as they left the library to join the guests in the hall. Ruben played a soft number as people chatted and mingled. Jillian thought he had upped his game for tonight.

With a loud meow, Possum ran up from behind Jillian and rubbed against her leg.

"Possum, how did you get out of Cornelia's room? You're a health code violation with food around." Jillian scooped up the cat, and, as she stood back up, the cat let out a sharp hiss in Flannery's direction. Jillian pulled him back, shocked he would do such a thing. "I'm so sorry. I don't know what is wrong with him. Let me get him back upstairs."

Flannery recoiled into her father's protective embrace. It appeared their disdain for each other was mutual. *But why?*

Jillian removed Possum to the kitchen and found Cornelia by the stairs. "Oh, there he is," Cornelia said. "He ran out when

I went upstairs to freshen up. He moved so fast, I couldn't catch him. Something spooked him."

"You can say that again. You should have seen the way he reacted to Flannery. He actually hissed at her."

Cornelia's eyes widened and Jillian could see the gears begin to turn in her great-aunt's brain. "He never hisses. What if—"

"Don't go there, Cornelia," Jillian warned under her breath as she passed Possum over to her. "Flannery is innocent in all this."

Isn't she?

Yes. Flannery Garland didn't have anything to do with killing Bo Tyler.

Cornelia clucked disbelievingly. "Raymond is rarely wrong about people."

Jillian reasoned further. "Flannery was tricked by Bo, and even cheated by her own mother when that woman set this ridiculous trust-fund requirement of marriage by twenty-six. Flannery needed Bo to fulfill it. Even if she did kill him, she wouldn't have done it before they were married and risk losing access to that trust fund. Especially so close to her deadline. Oh, that's an unfortunate word at the moment, isn't it?"

Cornelia seemed to consider Jillian's words, but her pursed lips told Jillian she wasn't ready to give up the idea yet. "She hit your car."

"Only because she was trying to scare me so I would back off. I think that's the reason, anyway." She hadn't brought up the incident with Flannery yet, figuring they could work it out after they fried their bigger fish—Devon.

"That's a pretty expensive message she was sending."

"I'm sure we'll get it worked out."

Cornelia sighed. "All I know is Raymond is intuitive. I have always trusted his instincts." She started up the steps, and Possum stared at Jillian over her shoulder, his eyes piercing. "Watch your back, dear."

"Jillian?" a voice called.

She whipped around to find Flannery heading her way.

"Is the kitty okay?" she asked.

Jillian gave the younger woman what she hoped was a warm smile. "He's just not used to so many strange people on his turf. He'll be fine upstairs, away from it all."

"Good. I mean, I'm glad he'll be happier up there."

As she ushered Flannery back to the hall, Jillian speculated as to why the beauty queen could possibly consider Possum a threat. Could it be more than an aversion to cats?

Ruben struck up a fun groove that filled Belle Haven to the rooftops and quickly brought the guests into the main hall from all directions. Conversation ceased as elegantly dressed people stopped sipping their drinks and found places to take in the show.

"I guess that's our cue to begin," Jillian said so that only Flannery could hear. "Ready to catch Bo's killer?"

"Someone has to pay, and it won't be me," Flannery said with a smile.

Jillian stalled. Like a swift punch, she was hit with the idea that she'd trusted the wrong person in orchestrating tonight's event.

Flannery paused and looked at Jillian curiously. "Get it? *I* won't be paying, since I won't have my trust fund, so Devon won't get a penny. Your plan was brilliant, Jillian. Thank you." Flannery blew Jillian an exaggerated kiss and floated away before Jillian could form an articulate word.

Have I been conned?

In the hall, Ruben transitioned into a rendition of "Take Five" as everyone assembled around the piano. When it ended, he welcomed the crowd. "Tonight is a night of celebration. Flannery Garland has accepted Devon Greer's wedding proposal. Has your young man arrived, Miss Flannery?" Ruben asked her as she stepped up to the piano and placed a hand on his shoulder.

"I do believe my love is here." She searched the crowd and smiled as the handsome Devon Greer entered the hall.

Ruben beamed. "I thought we might ease into the night with 'Summertime.' Sound good?"

"Sounds blissful. After all, it is summertime, and the living is easy. Take it away, Ruben."

The piano keys began a slow few notes before Flannery's robust voice brought goosebumps to the bared arms of the ladies and smiles to the gentlemen. Earle had been correct. His daughter had plenty of talent. It was no wonder she'd been successful on the pageant circuit. She was beautiful, gifted, and completely mesmerizing.

Jillian found herself enthralled, remembering the night at the fund-raiser when Flannery had sung her heart out with Jeremiah accompanying her. The two were fantastic together. Bo had been furious at seeing his fiancée performing with his enemy, never mind that they were exceptional together. At the time, he'd looked as though he could commit murder. If Jillian didn't know better, she might say Flannery had been trying to entice a brawl.

Then Flannery had run off, leading Bo away from Jeremiah and the crowd. Leading him out into the garden . . . to the place where he had died. It made Jillian wonder whether Flannery was as talented an actress as she was a singer.

Flannery's voice rose to a crescendo. Jillian realized she hadn't taken a breath in a while when her chest ached and her head swam. She stepped back and hit someone behind her.

"Whoa, careful. You'll bowl the guests over." Hunter's voice met her ear.

She whirled around and whispered, "Hunter, did Flannery know Bo would be killed? What if she led him straight to his death?"

"What makes you say that?"

Jillian bit her lower lip. "For one thing, Possum acts like he doesn't like her."

Hunter smiled. "Well, if Possum doesn't like her she must be guilty."

"You don't understand. He actually hissed at her." Jillian gasped as an idea struck her. "He must have seen her sneaking on the property to put that warning note on my door. That's got to be it."

"Maybe, maybe not. The night's young."

"You're right. I'm jumping the gun."

"Hey, no more guns," Hunter said seriously. He glanced over Jillian's shoulder. "He seems pleased with his future bride."

Jillian followed his gaze to see that Devon stood in the doorway admiring his bride-to-be with a slight smile on his face that could only mean true love.

Devon adored Flannery, Jillian realized. He wasn't using her for her money.

Flannery's part of the song ended, and Ruben played a bit more before finishing with an elaborate riff that brought everyone closer to him, their applause thunderous and appreciative. Words of affirmation spread through the room.

"That was wonderful."

"Breathtaking."

"I'm in awe."

"Bravo!"

Flannery curtsied and beamed at the adoring crowd. "Thank you all for coming. It's been a harrowing time since Sterling's death, and I've done a lot of reflecting on the path I want my future to take." She glanced in Devon's direction. Jillian watched him move to step into the spotlight with her, but Flannery shook her head slightly. "As many of you know, my mother passed away when I was sixteen. She worried I would live a frivolous life and made a silly stipulation in the trust she put aside for me." Flannery laughed, but the crowd grew confused at the oddly personal revelation. Clearly, they were wondering what her trust had to do with her engagement.

Jillian tightened her grip on Hunter's hand.

Flannery continued. "I mention this because, you see, if I'm not married before I turn twenty-six, I can't access the money my mother left for me. I thought I would be fine because Sterling had asked me to marry him, but in just a few days, I'll be twenty-six, and now I will never see that money."

Some of the crowd craned their necks to find Devon. Blatant stares his way caused him to laugh nervously.

"News to me," he said jokingly.

"I've decided I'm not going to marry you until after I turn twenty-six—if you'll still have me, that is."

"I'll marry you whenever you want. However you want. I love you," Devon said without hesitation. "I've always loved you."

"Perhaps you didn't hear me correctly. I said I'd marry you *after* my birthday. You do understand what that means, don't you?"

"Give me some credit," Devon said with a smile. "I'm pretty good with numbers."

"So then you know how much money you'll be getting from me."

"Not a cent. And that's fine. I don't need it."

Flannery frowned. She searched the crowd until she found Jillian.

This was not how they had planned for the evening to go. Devon was supposed to become angry at losing the fortune he thought would be his.

But the man seemed perfectly happy without it.

Flannery stamped her foot. "Well, I don't love you. I could never love you, and you know why."

The crowd stilled, enthralled by this strange turn of events.

Devon closed his eyes and sighed, then opened them again and gazed earnestly at Flannery. "It's not what you think," he said. "I did what I had to because I loved you. And I love you still."

"You love my money," she snapped.

Devon stepped up to the piano. "Excuse me, Ruben. I'm going to need that seat."

Ruben slid out from behind the piano with help from a man standing nearby.

Devon tested the sound of the keys and played a quick warm-up chord. Jillian didn't realize he could play, and judging by some interested faces around her, she wasn't the only one surprised.

Flannery was still livid, however. "I already told you I won't marry you before my birthday, so don't try to convince me."

Devon moved into a song, seemingly ignoring her. "Remember this one, sweetheart? We used to play this one together all the time. Come on, sing along. Show everyone how good we are together."

Flannery shook her head. "Why are you doing this? I'm not getting the money!"

"Great. It will go to a good cause."

"This doesn't make any sense."

"Sure it does. Think about it."

"You're a crook."

"You were going to marry another crook, Flannery. And he was in it for the cash. I want to marry you, money or no money."

When Flannery stood by without singing a word, Devon began singing the Frank Sinatra song "My One and Only Love" with such heart Jillian found herself choking up.

"Stop it!" Flannery cried, her voice cracking. Devon's attempt to sway her seemed to be working. Flannery actually did love him. "Just stop it," she sputtered, a last-ditch effort to push him away.

Devon played on, but stopped singing. "I can't," he said evenly, "and I won't. Not ever. I will always love you."

Jillian suddenly wondered if Bo Tyler's death was a crime of passion. Would Devon kill him out of jealousy? She put her free hand to her forehead. She was getting dizzy with the constantly changing what-ifs buzzing around her brain.

Devon continued singing the bluesy love song. Flannery swiped a hand across her cheeks. A survey of the room showed others were also moved to tears as well.

All except for one.

Jillian dropped her gaze to keep from gawking at Earle Garland's enraged face, his wound flaming red.

"Please, Devon, don't do this," Flannery pleaded. "I could never marry you, not after what you've done."

"Everything I did, I did for you. I worked hard and rose up the ladder to CEO to be worthy of you. We have your father's blessing now. Everything will work out. All debts have been paid."

"Not while an innocent man sits in a prison cell for a murder he didn't commit."

Devon frowned and his piano playing stopped. "What does that have to do with us?"

"You killed Sterling," Flannery said emphatically and ran toward the front of the house.

Devon jumped to his feet, his face awash in shock as the music abruptly ended. He moved to go after her, but Hunter stepped up and put a hand on his forearm.

"The last man to go after her like that didn't survive. You'd best stay put."

"But I didn't kill anyone!" Devon scanned the room of shocked faces. He stopped on Earle Garland. "Tell them, sir. Tell them I would never do such a thing."

"I know no such thing," Earle replied. "Your poor track record at Fugue Labs precedes you."

"But none of that is my fault. It was yours. I covered for you. I've always been covering for *you*."

"I don't know what you're talking about. You're clearly confused." Earle grew flustered, his face still red. "Now, if you'll excuse me, I need to go find my daughter. You're to stay away from her from here on. You've done enough damage."

"You mean I didn't do enough, don't you, Garland?" Devon demanded.

Earle paused in midstep, then started walking again—faster, Jillian thought.

Devon continued to hurl accusations at the man. "I made all the excuses for you once before, when Fugue Labs started failing, and I lost Flannery over it. You promised you would fix everything, but you lied. Nothing's been fixed. And now she thinks I killed Sterling. Why would that be? How could you do this to me? To us?"

Earle had made it to the door when everything clicked for Jillian. Before she could stop herself, she yelled, "Don't let him leave. He killed Bo Tyler!"

Earle swung around. "How dare you suggest such a thing!"

Jillian wanted to shrink back, but Hunter's nod of approval kept her strong and sure. "It all makes sense," she said. "Your daughter's birthday was approaching, and she had chosen someone who was using her. You knew it and couldn't have that. Because you knew he would take her money and skip town, leaving you with nothing to take from her yourself. You're just as bad as he was—no, worse, because you were going to steal from your own daughter. You also owed Devon because he'd covered for you when you were embezzling from Fugue Labs with Bo. It wasn't Devon and Bo working together. It was you and Bo. You knew if you could get rid of Bo before Flannery's birthday, she would have to marry Devon to receive her money, which I'm sure you planned to oversee. Especially since you are out of money and can't afford to keep your house staffed." Jillian took a breath. "And the cut didn't come from Devon, did it?"

Devon choked. "You pinned that on me too?"

Earle sneered at Devon. "Flannery gave it to me when I told her she had to marry you. She despises you and always will."

Jillian saw the lie at once. "No, you gave it to yourself to put others off your trail." *How could someone be so selfish?*

Devon's lip curled. Jillian thought he might go for Earle's throat if Hunter let go of him.

Earle spoke to the room. "Now, if you all will excuse me. I've had enough of your speculations. I do not have to stand here and listen to them."

"Perhaps you'll listen to me." Lucinda stepped into the fray. "Earle, I can't believe what I am hearing right now. Jeremiah is innocent, yes, but there must be a mistake."

Earle puffed up his chest. "Jeremiah is not innocent. He's a thief who can't mind his own business. Not to mention his bleeding heart for widows and orphans. His contacting you was his worst mistake, and now he'll pay for it forever."

Lucinda inhaled in shock, her hand over her heart. "It *was* you. You did this to me? You stole from me?"

"Not enough," Earle snarled, apparently finally accepting that he wouldn't be getting out of this situation unscathed.

Gooder, dressed in a tuxedo, stepped out from behind a potted fern with handcuffs in hand. "Earle Garland, you are under arrest for the murder of Bo Tyler, and apparently a host of other crimes."

"What?" Confusion washed over his face as more officers stepped near as backup. "You're making a big mistake." Earle yanked away, and in the next second, a gun appeared in his right hand. "Stay back!" he shouted to the crowd.

People screamed. Many ducked through the nearest doorway in a frenzy.

Unlike the gun she'd faced down the other day, Jillian was sure this one was loaded.

Earle grabbed Lucinda with his free hand. He yanked her back against him with one arm around her neck and put the gun to her head. "Let me out of here, or I will shoot her."

A horrified silence fell over the room as spectators watched Earle drag Lucinda to the exit. Even the officers who'd been ready to make a routine arrest mere moments before didn't dare make a move on Earle.

"How could you, Earle?" Lucinda cried. "Alan loved you like a brother. And you stole from him. You stole from me." With that, the proper, ladylike Lucille lifted her foot and brought her high heel down on Earle's instep.

The man howled. Lucinda jabbed backward, slamming her dainty elbow into Earle's nose. Blood spurted out and Earle roared in rage and pain. Then he realized Lucinda had escaped his grasp. He lifted his gun and aimed it at her.

The next second, he crumpled to the ground.

Annalise stood behind him. She held what was left of a porcelain vase from the entryway table. The last Sweetie Pie had finally arrived.

"Sorry, I'm late," she said calmly. "Byron was stuck at the bank. He's parking the car now."

Bertie hooted. "This is the first time I am glad he has been working such late hours. Annalise, you saved the day."

Byron Reed walked in with a distraught Flannery in the crook of his arm. He fixed his attention on Devon, who was still held back by Hunter. "Son, this lady says she belongs to you—if you'll still have her." Byron nudged Flannery toward Devon, and then he and Annalise exchanged loving smiles. "My advice to you is that you never let her go again. I don't know what I would do if I lost my bride."

Annalise reached for her husband's arm. "Oh, Byron, you don't ever have to worry about such a thing."

Hunter released Devon, who ran to envelope Flannery in his arms. Motherless already, the poor girl had now essentially lost her father, and Jillian knew she'd need all the support Devon and Lucinda could muster.

As the authorities moved in to secure the scene and take Earle away, the Sweetie Pies gathered close to Jillian, issuing exclamations of relief that, although it hadn't gone quite as planned, the evening had had the desired outcome of discovering Bo Tyler's real killer.

"It's finished," Jillian said with no small amount of relief. "Jeremiah will be free, and the right man will finally be behind bars."

"I figured it out ages ago," Cornelia claimed, as if she hadn't been telling Jillian that Flannery was behind it all barely an hour before.

"I knew you could do it the whole time," Hunter said as he came up behind Jillian. "Wasn't worried for a minute."

"Speak for yourself," grumbled Bertie. "I've been jumpy as a cat on a hot tin roof."

Jillian put an arm around her shoulders. "Well, it's over now. We can leave all the feline behavior to Possum."

Brass instruments honked and squeaked in a joyful cacophony. Students with crisp white shirts and pressed black pants tried out their new instruments, warming up for their upcoming performance. The saxophones, trumpets, trombones, and tubas gleamed bright in the summer afternoon sun warming Moss Hollow's downtown square.

The brick streets were closed off to vehicle traffic so that townsfolk could gather to hear the band. They'd be performing the same numbers that had garnered them the championship title in the national competition.

For several days, the Sweetie Pies had prepared for the celebratory festival, and they had outdone themselves. A stage had been set up on the lawn, and bunches of red, white, and blue balloons decorated the front and sides. The Sweetie Pies were attending a series of long tables full of every kind of treat imaginable, and everyone in Moss Hollow had come out to eat and show support.

As she surveyed the joyful scene from near one of the dessert tables, Jillian reached for Hunter's hand.

"Think I can finally have that dance today?" he asked.

"Nothing would make me happier," Jillian said, checking the time. "Only a few more minutes until showtime."

"Say cheese!" Savannah held her cell phone up in front of Jillian and Hunter, startling them. After the phone issued its digitized *click*, Savannah checked the screen. "Aw, how sweet. You two are adorable." She raced off to take Annalise and Byron's photo next. The long-married couple held hands on a street bench, and Jillian was glad to see that the recent stress seemed to have evaporated from their relationship.

"I hope it was a good picture," Jillian said to Hunter. "I feel like she caught me with a weird look on my face."

"I'm sure you're beautiful in it."

Jillian felt her cheeks warm. "You're just saying that because you want my raspberry almond scones."

"Scones may have a little to do with it, but I do think you're beautiful. And smart. And brave."

"Ain't that the truth." Jeremiah Davis had appeared beside them. "I wasn't eavesdropping, but I did catch the part about you being brave." He beamed at her. "I am forever in your debt, Miss Jillian."

Jillian waved away his words, embarrassed. "Don't be silly. I only did what anyone would."

Jeremiah laughed and shook his head. "I've been around long enough to know you are a rare gem. I can't tell you how much I appreciate the risks you took for me. Thank you."

Mia and Paulie joined them. When Jeremiah saw them, he smiled and put one arm around each. He tousled Paulie's hair and planted a kiss on Mia's cheek.

Jillian wondered if Mia's pretty blush meant romance could be on the horizon for the single mother and the piano man. Surely Paulie would welcome the idea—he already seemed to have plenty of affection for his neighbor and piano teacher.

"I'm so glad the charges were dropped," Jillian said to Jeremiah.

"I'm lucky Mr. Garland admitted to planting that wallet in my car," he said. "I've done things I'm not proud of in the past, sure, but I'm certainly thankful I won't be paying for something I didn't even do."

"Between framing you, leaving me that note, and tailing me and trying to run me off the road in Beech Brook, Earle sure did his best not to get caught." Jillian had realized after the party that Possum's hiss was aimed at Earle rather than Flannery. The cat had clearly been onto something. "Anyway, he'll be going away for a long time now that he's in police custody where he belongs."

"So, now that you're free, what's next for you, Jeremiah?" Hunter asked. "More traveling gigs?"

"Nah, I'm getting myself a day job." He tugged Mia even closer. "Mia put in a good word for me at her workplace, and I was officially hired this week. Sounds like things might be turning around at Fugue Labs now that they've patched the leak in their bank accounts."

Jillian smiled at the news, wondering if Lucinda Atwood had also had a say in his new position. "Good for you, Jeremiah. But please don't ever stop playing the piano."

"Impossible. It's in my blood. And Mr. Greer understands if I work some nights at Ken's." Jeremiah nodded toward the stage.

Jillian looked over to see Devon, his arm draped around the new Mrs. Greer. They seemed blissfully in love, neither of them caring one bit that delaying their marriage had cost them a whole lot of money. Just as Flannery had said at the party, every penny of her trust fund had been given away. Thankfully, she had been able to decide which good cause would benefit. She had chosen the local school's music program—providing the new instruments and uniforms currently in use by the happy, talented teenagers on the stage—and had also set up scholarship funds for students going on to study music.

Flannery and Devon stepped on stage to address the crowd. Clearly comfortable speaking to large groups, Flannery smiled and grabbed the microphone. "Welcome, everyone. We are so proud of Moss Hollow's young musicians, and we know this is only the beginning for them."

Devon leaned toward the mic. "Music brings people from all backgrounds together. I hope you kids, and you in the audience as well, will let it lead you into friendships that last a lifetime."

Flannery beamed up at her husband, and Jillian knew Flannery had truly married for love.

"Let's get this party started!" Flannery yelled, and the crowd cheered. The band pushed out the beginning notes of a song, and people began to dance.

Jeremiah peered at Mia shyly. "You wouldn't want—I mean . . ." He took a deep breath and blurted, "Would you care to dance? With me, I mean?"

Mia blushed and nodded. "I would love that."

"You would?" Jeremiah looked surprised that he hadn't been turned down.

"Yes," Mia replied and led him closer to the band.

Jeremiah glanced back and said as he walked away, "Thank you, Miss Green. No one has ever done anything like that for me before."

Jillian called back, "They should have."

Jeremiah's humble smile would stay with Jillian forever. Maybe if someone had extended a hand to him earlier he wouldn't have turned to crime to get ahead. Regardless, he'd been given a second chance at an honest life. Judging by the way he gazed at the woman in his arms, he was off to a good start.

Jillian faced Paulie. "I think your mom has turned Jeremiah's head. What do you think?" At the boy's devious smile, suddenly it clicked. "Paulie, why do I think you have been playing matchmaker? You don't actually care about learning to play piano, do you?"

Paulie shrugged, then surveyed the dessert tables. "I like it well enough, but you adults are so blind. Sometimes it's hard work to get you to open your eyes and see what is right in front of you. I was starting to worry that Mom and J.D. would never get the hint. Are those more of your chocolate chip cookies over there? I'm hungry." The boy disappeared into the crowd.

"Oh to be so young and unaware of how complicated life can be," Jillian said.

"Right," Hunter admitted with a nod. "Complicated. He'll find out one day just how hard it is to tell someone how you feel about them."

Before Jillian could respond, she heard a tentative throat clearing. She turned to see Virginia Porter, who was on the arts commission board with Lucinda. "Jillian, you and your girls have done just a wonderful job with this event," the older woman said.

"Thank you so much." Jillian smiled. "I know it's not quite as grand as the event at Jardin d'Amandes."

"No, but it's a lot safer." The older woman chuckled. "It's so nice to see these children happy and successful. And it's a relief to put that whole messy business behind us."

"Yes, it is. Although, if you don't mind me asking, was it Flannery who stopped you on the street outside the salon that day?"

Virginia shook her head. "Heavens, no. It was Earle Garland in her car, and he was in a right foul mood. He and Alton liked to play poker together, and he'd recently lost a fair amount of money to my Alton. I didn't realize how much, exactly, until it came out about the Garlands being quite penniless after all."

"Yes, it shocked a lot of people," Jillian said.

"Anyway, Earle gave me an earful about Alton being a cheat and a scoundrel and so forth. It was difficult to listen to, especially since it isn't true. Earle just made some poor decisions. Alton knows what he's doing at the tables, and he never risks more than he can afford, which is why I don't have a problem with it." She waved a hand. "All in the past now, of course. Although, Alton felt so poorly for that young piano player sitting in jail that he's hired him for our fiftieth wedding anniversary party next month. I'll be dancing the whole night."

"I can't think of anything better." Jillian smiled. "It seems like it all worked out in the end."

"It did indeed. Take care now, sweetheart."

As Virginia walked away, another familiar face appeared. "Mrs. Coleman, how nice to see you," Jillian said as two blonde women approached. "And this must be Paige."

"Hello, Jillian," Mrs. Coleman said with a smile. "Paige, this is the baker I was telling you about."

"It's so nice to meet you," Paige said, flashing a megawatt smile and shaking Jillian's hand. "My mom told me about your—what do you call them?—sugared magnolias, and they sound totally adorable. Graham and I are so lucky she's planning the wedding for us. She has the best taste ever, so I know those little flowers will be just perfect. I can't wait to see them."

Jillian raised an eyebrow. "Does this mean we'll be making your wedding cake?"

"Mom!" Paige put her left hand to her forehead, nearly blinding Jillian with her engagement ring. The breathtaking diamond rivaled Flannery's in scale and brilliance. Apparently the two were on an even playing field now. "We should have signed the contract ages ago. I don't want her slipping out of our fingers to do someone else's cake that weekend."

"Don't worry," Jillian said with a smile. "I'm all yours."

"Aren't you all mine?" Hunter murmured as mother and daughter moved on.

"Doesn't that go without saying?" she answered with a grin.

A pair of young girls who appeared to be sisters approached the table. "Do you have any cupcakes with pink frosting?" the younger one asked.

"Are you just going to lick the frosting off like always?" The older sister was twelve going on thirty, it would seem. "That's so immature."

"It just so happens I have one pink cupcake left," Jillian said, handing it to the young girl.

"And what would you like?" Hunter asked the older sister.

"I don't need anything, thank you." The girl's posture remained stiff.

"Nothing?" Hunter acted taken aback. "Are you sure I can't tempt you with a cookie?" He gestured toward some oversize snickerdoodles.

"Nope." She lifted her nose haughtily.

"Maybe a turtle brownie?"

"No thank you." The girl folded her arms.

Hunter rubbed his chin and sent Jillian a wink. His confidence had yet to wane. "I've got it. Nothing too sweet for you." He reached across the table and lifted one of Jillian's raspberry almond scones. "These are my favorite. They go great with coffee. I mean, normally I would say they aren't for kids, so maybe you wouldn't like it. But you seem pretty grown up."

Jillian could tell he was trying so hard not to smile, and she bit back her own grin.

"I suppose I could try it," the girl said.

"Excellent." Hunter plucked up a napkin and a scone, then passed it over to her. "And I think I'll join you in having one. I've been looking forward to this ever since I heard they would be served today."

Hunter picked up his own and took a generous bite at the same time the girl did.

"Well, what do you think?" Jillian asked, even though it seemed rather obvious that the girl approved.

"Mmmm!" was the young lady's response.

Hunter threw the last bite into his mouth. "I think I'm in love."

Jillian did a double take. "What?"

"Yep," he said. "With these scones." He winked.

Jillian couldn't argue with that. They were delicious, if she did say so herself.

Two Birds With One Scone
Book Sixteen Recipe

Raspberry Almond Scones
Scones

2 cups all-purpose flour
1 tablespoon baking powder
3 tablespoons sugar
½ teaspoon salt
6 tablespoons cold, unsalted butter, cut into small cubes

1 cup plus 1 tablespoon heavy cream, divided
¼ teaspoon almond extract
⅓ cup sliced almonds
1 cup frozen raspberries

Almond Glaze

1 cup confectioner's sugar
4 tablespoons heavy cream or milk

½ teaspoon almond extract
¼ cup sliced almonds, for garnish

Instructions

Preheat oven to 400 degrees. Line a large baking sheet with parchment paper or a silicone mat and set aside.

1. To make scones, whisk together flour, baking powder, sugar, and salt in a large bowl. Cut in the butter using your hands, two knives, or a pastry blender. Mix until mixture resembles coarse meal. Alternatively, you can place these ingredients in a food processor and pulse until the coarse meal consistency is achieved, then pour the mixture into a large bowl.

2. Stir in 1 cup of heavy cream and almond extract until dough begins to form, but don't overmix. Gently fold in sliced almonds and raspberries (frozen raspberries hold their shape better).

3. Transfer dough to a lightly floured surface and knead by hand just until dough forms a ball. Form scones by patting the dough

into a ¾-inch-thick circle. Cut into eight even triangles and place on prepared baking sheet.

4. Using a pastry brush, brush scones lightly with 1 tablespoon heavy cream. Bake for 15 to 18 minutes, or until light brown. Cool on a wire cooling rack.

5. To make almond glaze, whisk together confectioner's sugar, heavy cream or milk, and almond extract until a drizzling consistency is reached. You may need to add up to an additional tablespoon of cream or milk. Drizzle glaze over the cooled scones. Toast sliced almonds for garnish, if desired, and then sprinkle over scones.

Yield: 8 servings.